A Regency Christmas Double

ROSIE CHAPEL

First printing 2018
This version 2023
ISBN: 978-0-6482797-9-2 (e-book)
ISBN: 978-0-6459731-4-3 (paperback)

Ulfire Pty. Ltd.
P.O. Box 1481
South Perth
WA 6951
Australia

www.rosiechapel.com

Cover Art: @nassyart and Canva elements.
Cover Designed by R Norman in Canva, using appropriate licences.

Acknowledgments

Thank you…

to Janet, Melody, Jackie, Julie, Amy and Lilly
your patience, love and support, as always, is invaluable.

to Graham from *A Fading Street Publishers* for his editing wizardry.

to my husband who, once upon a time, rescued my heart!

To all who believe in the magic of Christmas!

Heart
Rescued

Prologue

DECEMBER 1814

Every year the Duke and Duchess of Hereford hosted a festive ball on Christmas Eve, and every year they featured a titillating item of entertainment with which to enthral their guests.

The ball was a gala event, all of Society was invited, and the evening's display was always something unexpected.

It might be the performance of a new piece of music, a scene from a play not yet in the theatres; perhaps a game, maybe some magic, a reading from the very latest fashionable novel, a ballet or a display by acrobats.

This year they would be presenting the waltz.

Previously judged *sinfully* decadent, recently, the waltz had been given the seal of approval by no less than the patronesses of Almacks — although, it must be noted, strict rules still applied. The Duchess, despite her rather aloof demeanour had been rebellious when a child, and her wild streak still lurked.

This manifested, not only in her cool disregard for protocol — insisting she be addressed as Lady Hereford by her charges, declaring she was neither her husband's mother, nor in her dotage — but also prompted her to seek out amusements guaranteed to scandalise the stuffier members of Society.

The waltz slotted into that category perfectly.

She had determined there would be ten ladies, the incomparables of the winter Season, to be partnered by the ten most eligible bachelors.

The ladies had been rehearsing most afternoons for two weeks, as had their gentleman partners, coming together — under close supervision — for half an hour of the end of each session.

All were enjoying it immensely and none would be surprised if, by the night of the ball, more than one couple was inclined to extend their partnership beyond a simple dance.

This particular afternoon, the group had only just arrived and were awaiting their taskmistress. Most were twittering about the latest gossip and, although practicing, were not really paying attention to their steps.

All seemed as normal, when the chamber orchestra, who had been warming up their instruments, stopped playing so abruptly, the ladies nearly tripped over one another. Bewildered, they glanced around to see a handsome woman, who looked more remote than usual, standing in the doorway of the opulent ballroom.

"Lady Hereford." They curtsied as one. The soft material of their dresses billowing as they sank towards the floor, pretty pastel hues evoking spring buds bursting into flower. Lady Hereford came forward, slowly.

She studied them for a moment, then said quietly, "I'm afraid I have some sad news to impart. I have just been informed, Lady Emmeline was thrown from her horse this morning and did not survive the fall."

The young ladies stared at their benefactor in shock, mouths hanging open in the most unladylike fashion. They had been wondering why Emmeline wasn't there; she was invariably early to practice. She was the brightest of them all. Always happy, nothing got her down. She could make even these interminable dance lessons fun.

Emmeline couldn't be dead, she just couldn't.

Taught from an early age to control extremes of emotion, the remaining nine confined themselves to muttering fretfully under their breath.

"Your Grace?" one of their number, Constance, ventured.

"Yes, Constance," cold blue eyes warmed slightly at the young woman's obvious nerves.

Constance hesitated.

"Come on girl, spit it out, I don't have all day."

"I have no desire to sound impertinent or insensitive, but… what about… do you… errm… should we…?" Constance ground to a halt, unsure how to phrase what they were all thinking.

"You wish to know whether we should still perform at the ball?"

Relieved nods all around.

"I think it is important we do, but 'tis too close to the performance to find a substitute for Emmeline. We shall leave the number at nine."

"What about Jasp… Lord Bramwell? He was her partner and they were… she was going…" Diana, another of their number, trailed off.

It was long known Lady Emmeline Fortescue and Jasper Ogilvie — Viscount Bramwell — were expected to wed this coming summer. Although no date had been set, the couple was inseparable, both families approving their courtship. A rather shy but affable gentleman, they all knew and liked him. Jasper would be devastated.

"All the more reason not to introduce another partner for Lord Bramwell, who will have little to be joyful about this Christmas." Lady Hereford said somewhat bracingly, unwilling to let her charges wallow.

"Now come on ladies, no time to stand about mourning. Emmeline would be most upset if you let all your hard work go to waste. You know how much she loved this dance."

Lady Hereford nodded to the musicians, and Mozart's beautiful melody filled the room. The duchess worked them hard, leaving little time to dwell on the tragedy and by the end of the afternoon she believed they were ready.

Chapter One

I n an elegant parlour, in a stately residence, not far from Hyde Park, a shadow — imperceptible to human eyes, unless you looked really closely — was bent double with mirth, watching one lady trying to teach her friend the, not particularly difficult, steps of the waltz.

Emmeline Fortescue, a ghost of almost four years, often graced this quiet home, willing her one-time suitor to live again.

Of course, he couldn't hear or see her, but occasionally he muttered her name in his sleep and she would stroke his cheek affectionately, while crooning a lullaby — it seemed to settle him.

Now she had decided enough was enough. He had hidden himself away far too long and although, at first, Emmeline was flattered he grieved for her, now she was just exasperated, and determined he would not use her death as an excuse to avoid Society.

Thankfully, she had the perfect ploy. The very ball at which she was supposed to dance four years previously... before that skittish mare tossed her, resulting in her premature death... was going to present the same waltz.

Lady Hereford — who still demanded Society use this title — possibly at the insistence of a rather pushy spirit, felt it time to reprise the performance, this time with ten couples as originally intended.

Emmeline knew who should be the one to draw her erstwhile beau out of his shell, but she had not been at all certain how to orchestrate it, until this afternoon.

Enter Lady Harriet Winterbourne, only daughter of the 3rd Earl of Conway. With her flaming red hair and flashing green eyes, Harriet was not regarded as conventionally beautiful. She was too tall for one thing and her patrician nose sported a smattering of freckles — *goodness no.*

Moreover, although Harriet, for the most part, behaved with decorum, she was known to flout convention. Her temper matched her hair and she could be quite sharp when riled up.

She loved to ride her horse astride, and preferred tramping through the fields and woods of her family's country estate, to any of the ladylike activities enjoyed by her friends.

She found endless pleasure helping to care for all manner of growing things, animal and plant alike, and could often be found strolling through the garden of her home, *barefoot — oh the horror.* Books were Harriet's solace, and she had amassed an eclectic collection, of which her Papa was proud and her Mama — resigned.

A simpering, vacuous beauty, Harriet was not. She was vivacious, outspoken and opinionated but, she was also cheerful, friendly and loyal and, to the astonishment of many of the *ton*, one of the most popular of her peers.

Despite, or maybe because of, these traits, she was considered an incomparable, which Lord and Lady Conway hoped might help their daughter make a good match. Harriet, although pleasant to all, showed no particular interest in any of the suitable gentlemen.

She did not want a good match, she wanted a, forget to breathe, utterly exhilarating, lose yourself in bliss, match and on that she remained characteristically resolute.

Emmeline, who had been interested to note that Harriet managed to get away with what others dared not risk, knew this young woman was the one to challenge, provoke and arouse the emotions her beloved had long since buried, and was probably the last best hope.

Today, Emmeline was observing Harriet's quite execrable efforts to learn the waltz, her amusement increasing in direct proportion to Harriet's frustration.

"That's it, I cannot master this ridiculous dance." Harriet dropped onto a convenient chair despondently. "You know I have two left feet. Why on earth Lady Hereford felt I was an appropriate inclusion to this year's display is beyond me. I would have done better had it been a fencing contest."

"Stop being such a defeatist. Come on, try again." Lady Joanna Ogilvie encouraged her friend, who was looking decidedly ruffled.

Fiery hair, no longer confined to its neat bun was curling around her head, the ribbons on her gown had come untied and, as she had kicked off her boots, complaining they pinched her feet, her delicate stockings would be lucky to last the day.

Harriet huffed a sigh and tried again.

As expected of a lady of her standing, Harriet was well versed in genteel pursuits. She could sew; play the piano and the violin, the former with some skill, the latter with enthusiasm. She could draw, after a fashion, and could talk about absolutely nothing for as long as was required of her.

Unfortunately, she could *not*, and had never been able to, dance.

Harriet knew the story about the first time Lady Hereford had chosen to feature this waltz at her acclaimed Christmas Eve Ball. It was four years past, when the waltz was still deemed risqué.

Ten couples had been chosen with utmost care.

That the ladies were already classed as diamonds of the first water was not enough. They must also demonstrate impeccable deportment, be capable of conducting an intelligent conversation in a charming manner, and… of course… possess the ability to dance.

The gentlemen had to be tall, handsome, and unmarried.

Emmeline Fortescue, one of the belles of every event during that year, was killed mere days before the ball. What made it more heartbreaking, was that Joanna's brother, Jasper, was expected to marry Emmeline and had been her partner for the performance.

Jasper Ogilvie, now the 6th Earl of Rochford following the untimely death of his father, had always been a reticent gentleman, even more so since Emmeline's death. He was rarely seen in public, confining himself to his club and the business of the Rochford estates.

Harriet, best friends with his sister, had known Jasper since childhood and never stood on ceremony with him — to the chagrin of her own family. She was one of few able to raise even the hint of a smile and refused to tiptoe around him in the months succeeding the accident.

Too many people began to avoid Jasper for fear of saying something, which might cause more upset or remind him of his lost love. Not so Harriet, who insisted he accompany them when Joanna and she went for long walks by the Thames or took an afternoon's carriage ride through one of the parks.

As Jasper retreated further into his shell, Harriet found it harder to persuade him, but she never gave up, even if her pestering annoyed him, it was better than no reaction at all.

Harriet had not seen Jasper for quite some time, because he had retired to Rochford Hall nestled in the Somerset countryside at the beginning of summer. Oddly, she missed him. Harriet delighted in the rather acerbic banter they shared — infrequent though it had become — for neither gave the other any quarter.

It was much more entertaining to discuss politics and the economy of the country, than the weather or the latest gossip, which was all anyone else seemed interested in.

Just as she was thinking this, heavy footsteps could be heard thudding down the stairs. Joanna flew to the door of the parlour, stuck her head out.

"Jasper, is that you?" she called.

There was a mumbled reply.

"Please come here, we need you."

Another grumble.

Joanna slipped into the hall and a brief argument, conducted in fierce undertones, ensued. Joanna reappeared her face slightly flushed and, on her heels, a lean and very tall gentleman, his lowered bows and mutinous expression testament to how glad he was to be there.

"Jasper, you remember Harry, don't you?" Knowing he did and without giving him chance to reply, she hurried on.

"Anyway she, or rather, we have been chosen to do this waltz. I know you hate this time of year and especially the Hereford's

Christmas Ball, but Harry is struggling with the steps and I am finding it hard to be the 'man.' Please, please help. You don't want Harry to make a fool of herself, do you?"

Widening her eyes and bestowing on him her most winsome smile, Joanna's entreaty looked to fall on deaf ears until her last words. Jasper looked annoyed, but as he glanced at Harriet, who was fidgeting uncomfortably, his expression softened.

"Are you trying to tell me, our sophisticated Lady Harriet Winterbourne can't dance?" Jasper bit his lip as, out of the blue, he wanted to laugh. Harriet always gave the impression of being so... well... accomplished.

Harriet glared at him, a deep red curl falling over her face. "Oh, so you think it amusing do you, my Lord? You cannot imagine how delighted I am to hear my incompetence brightens your otherwise boring day." Unsure why his comment prompted such churlishness, Harriet decided it was high time she took her leave.

She was tired, and aggravated that a simple dance step was beyond her, and her temper — as fiery as her hair — was wont to spill over without warning.

"Thank you for everything, Joanna. Mayhap we might try again soon, although we have yet another rehearsal tomorrow." Her tone indicating her distinct lack of enthusiasm. "Perhaps, Lady Hereford will see I am a lost cause and allow me to withdraw." She sat down to pull on her boots, when a deep voice spoke.

"Lady Harriet."

She paused and looked up. Jasper took a stride towards her, opening his palms in a gesture of apology.

"I beg your pardon, my lady. I had no mind to be insensitive. I was simply astonished there was something at which you are not skilled."

Harriet sat back in the chair and stared at him suspiciously, searching his face to see whether he spoke in jest.

"I should be honoured to teach you."

She was not convinced.

"Truly." He held her gaze for long moments.

About to tell him not to bother, something in his eyes stopped her and Harriet found herself nodding instead.

She finished lacing up her boots and stood, brushing out her skirts. "Thank you, my lord. I would appreciate it. I do not wish to encroach on your day, however, so perhaps we ought to arrange a more convenient time."

"My day has nothing pressing. If you have a little time now, maybe we should make a start?"

"If you are sure, I would be grateful. Might I suggest you change into sturdier shoes, otherwise your feet will likely be black and blue," she suggested, dubiously.

"I think you will find my shoes are quite sturdy enough, my lady. Now, Joanna, would you be so kind as to play for us?"

Joanna nodded and slid into the seat at the piano, her slim fingers caressing the cool ivory.

Jasper motioned for Harriet to come closer; she hesitated, then remembered Joanna was there, and as a pale pink blush washed up her face, moved into his arms.

Chapter Two

E mmeline watched, nodding her head in approval as, with utmost patience, Jasper explained the steps of the dance.

"The easiest way, is to imagine there is a square on the floor. Your feet should stop at the corners of the square, slide along the edges and then move diagonally across the centre of the box. Like this…"

Jasper demonstrated on his own, then took Harriet into his arms and they tried it together. While it took several attempts, gradually, she began to understand the movement.

"Counting the steps might help too. The rhythm is three beats… 1-2-3, 1-2-3. If we count the rhythm twice, we should have completed the box. Try it."

Harriet shut her eyes and concentrated, but could not get her head and her feet to work in unison. After treading on Jasper's toes, for the umpteenth time, she pulled away.

"My apologies, Lord Jasper, although to be fair, I did warn you." She spread her hands deprecatingly. "Thank you for trying to help, but I do not think I shall ever be able to dance." Her lovely face fell. "I know I'm going to let everyone down. Joanna and the other girls are all experts. 'Tis only me spoiling it."

"Lady Harriet, please do not be so defeatist," Unknowingly, Jasper echoed his sister's words. "By the evening of the ball you will be as adept at the waltz as though born to dance it. Now come on, one more time."

He grinned at Joanna who began to play a composition by Mozart. Harriet loved Mozart; his music had the ability to transport her. Taking a breath, she let Jasper lead and tried to follow.

Jasper Ogilvie stared down at the woman in his arms. Her eyes were shut, dark lashes a smutty curve on her creamy cheeks. Pale reddish-brown freckles sprinkled across a nose he was beset with a sudden urge to kiss.

Wait... what? No! He had no interest in Harriet. She was just his sister's pesky friend. He shook his head, banishing the thought and concentrated on making sure Harriet did not bruise any more of his poor toes.

Emmeline frowned. It was going to take a little more encouragement, but she believed the seeds had been sown. The ball was in a fortnight, plenty of time to let them flourish, they just needed the right kind of nourishment to bloom.

Harriet thanked Jasper, dropping a neatly executed curtsy, apologising once again for stamping on his toes.

"I appreciate you taking the time to help, but as you can see, 'tis pointless. I shall speak with Lady Hereford and request she find someone less incompetent." Harriet shrugged into a heavy winter cloak and slipped her hands into a fur-lined muff.

Jasper blinked. The rich forest green of her cloak was the perfect complement to her hair, which clung to the hood like flames. She fair took his breath away. He dragged his attention back to her and heard himself say,

"Please do not be hasty. If Joanna is agreeable, and you are prepared to come each morning, at say eleven, I would be happy to tutor you in the waltz." His head castigated him for offering to assist in so fruitless a task, while his heart thudded at her grateful smile.

Joanna clapped her hands, gleefully. "Do say you will, Harry. Thank you, Jasper." Flinging her arms around her brother, she gave him a bear hug.

Jasper chuckled and unwound Joanna's arms from his neck. "'Tis naught, a half hour here and there and you will be as proficient as your friends. Now, I must go. I was on my way to attend something, before you diverted me."

Frowning, he tried to recall what had prompted him to come past the parlour.

He bowed. "I look forward to our next lesson, Lady Harriet."

"As do I, and please call me Harriet. 'Tis ridiculous, 'lady' this and 'lady' that when you are teaching me the waltz. Goodness, you just held my hand," Harriet entreated, her face lighting up in an engaging grin.

Jasper felt the most peculiar sensation, as though the ground was undulating beneath him. He tried to speak, swallowed, and tried again.

"Only if you might agree to calling me Jasper?" His voice

sounded raspy even to his own ears, but he held her gaze until she inclined her head in agreement.

"Until tomorrow then," he managed, and walked out, Joanna's clarion tones following him as he strode across the hall to the front door.

"I knew he would help. 'Tis about time Jasper smiled again, he used to be so much fun…"

The rest of her sentence was lost as the door swung closed, but Jasper paused, grimacing. *Was he a grouch? No, of course he wasn't.* He had taken less than four steps when her words repeated themselves in his head and a face swam over his vision.

Emmeline.

It was a long time since Jasper had allowed himself to think of her. Initially it was too painful, and then it was easier not to remember. Jasper had loved Emmeline, but one of the reasons he shut himself away after her death, was guilt.

He had not loved her with a burning passion; he had loved her with a gentle tenderness. Yes, they would have had a happy union, but it would have been a quiet happiness.

Once the initial shock diminished, Jasper admitted inwardly that his life hadn't been unduly affected. Of course, they hadn't been married, so there was not the issue of an empty house or motherless children, but he had expected to feel more… well… desolate, lost, gut-wrenchingly heartbroken, when all he felt was sad.

Unable to deal with the well-wishers, Jasper withdrew. Presuming him to be prostrated with grief, everyone left him alone, and he became a recluse.

Now someone, entirely unexpectedly and in so short a time, had begun to chip away at his armour. Emmeline's face vanished, and another insinuated itself into his mind.

Harriet's lively countenance, her captivating eyes and blazing hair, the hint of vulnerability at not being able to dance; these things swirled around his head, no matter how hard he tried to shove them aside. Harriet was out of his league; he was years older and imagined she saw him simply as Joanna's brother. He suspected she had young bucks hanging off her every word — handsome, wealthy bachelors offering more than he ever could.

Jasper was endlessly amazed that Emmeline had agreed to his suit. He was taller and thinner than was deemed fashionable — lanky was the less than polite term often used; Emmeline, a petite young woman, barely reaching his shoulders. His features were craggy rather than handsome and, since childhood, whenever nervous, or uncomfortable, he retreated behind a gruff veneer, which could seem forbidding.

Emmeline was, had been, stunningly beautiful, blessed with grace and poise, in fact, the epitome of a diamond. She could have had any man she wanted, yet she chose him. Despite guessing it was because, with him, she felt safe, Jasper had been flattered and the more time they spent together the more content they were.

Marriage was the logical progression, and neither fought against the desires of their parents when a union was suggested.

Then the idyll was shattered and, during these last four years, he had maintained an emotionless façade. To his disquiet, Jasper had the niggling suspicion Lady Harriet Winterbourne was about to turn his unruffled life into a chaotic mess.

Emmeline felt less perturbed. This was working out just fine.

Over the next few days, Harriet presented herself promptly at eleven.

Jasper, who had found a stout pair of boots and thick woollen stockings to protect his feet, discovered, to his amazement, these half-hour lessons to be quite agreeable.

Joanna played the piano, while Jasper led Harriet through the finer points of the waltz.

In the short breaks they took, the three chatted. Nothing of any real consequence, just snippets of their lives, but something began to blossom between Jasper and Harriet, subtle but tangible — to the relief of a certain ghost!

Emmeline was correct; Harriet challenged Jasper at every turn. While they shared many opinions, Harriet took mischievous delight in questioning Jasper's observations concerning the social and political climate of England; the two falling back into the stimulating debates they used to enjoy before he shut himself away.

Once Harriet had mastered the square, Jasper added to her confusion by saying they needed to include a turn. Then, to make matters worse, talked about the rise and fall, and that one was expected to take long gliding steps.

On the first step forward, the weight should be on the heel, lifting to the ball of the foot with a gradual rise to the toes — starting at the first beat and continuing through the second to the start of the third; lowering to normal position by the end of the third beat.

Harriet gaped at Jasper when he explained this. There was far too much counting and turning and rising and falling. How on earth did one manage to maintain their rhythm?

Joanna was reduced to helpless laughter by Harriet's contortions, she always went the opposite way from Jasper's instructions tying herself, not to mention Jasper, into knots.

Despite all sensible arguments to the contrary, Harriet persevered, but even her most ardent supporter would have been hard-pressed to say she was any closer to grasping the minutiae of the waltz.

Chapter Three

One morning, several days after their first lesson, and in the middle of practice, Harriet stopped abruptly and went to sit on one of the leather chairs by the large bay window.

She stared out over the garden, chewing her lip. This was hopeless, it did not matter what she did, her brain and her feet refused to cooperate.

"Harriet?" Joanna's soft question engendered no response. She looked at her brother, he looked at her and they both shrugged, perplexed.

"Harriet." Jasper's deeper tones caused Harriet to turn around, the room coming back into focus.

"I cannot do this. I know you have tried but as you can see it is a complete waste of everyone's time. I am sorry to have diverted your attention from what were likely far more important matters, to attempt to transform me into someone, plainly, I am not."

Her voice was quiet, empty of inflection and so unlike Harriet, the siblings glanced at each other again, nonplussed.

"I shall tell Lady Hereford this afternoon that once again, it will be only nine couples. Mayhap this waltz *is* cursed." This last almost a whisper.

Jasper was visited by the bizarre notion that should Harriet stop coming for lessons, his world would be less bright. Even with her remarkable lack of skill, and his very sore feet, he had enjoyed these last few days. He would miss her vivid face, her sparkling eyes glimmering with laughter, and the feel of her in his arms — which was sublime.

For reasons he had not yet grasped, he needed to persuade her to continue.

"Harriet, come now, this isn't like you. Moreover, 'tis unfair on the gentleman with whom you are partnered, to pull out now. I did not take you for one to give up when things are tough," he spoke bracingly and watched her expression morph from melancholy to obstinate.

"I imagine you would be glad to see the end of this farce. I daresay your feet will be forever in my debt if we stop now, never mind that I know how difficult this must be for you. I saw how it affected you the first time. Remember? You do not need my ineptitude to drag it all back up again," Harriet retorted.

She ignored Joanna's sharp intake of breath. No one ever discussed Emmeline with Jasper, which Harriet thought absurd. How was he supposed to move on if he was never able to vent his grief?

He should have been encouraged to talk about Emmeline, every day, until he could do so without experiencing an all-consuming sorrow.

Although Harriet hadn't known Emmeline personally, they moved in the same circles, and she was always struck by the other girl's zest for life. She did not float through it serenely; she hurled herself at it with verve. Harriet suspected Emmeline might want to slap Jasper for hiding himself away.

As this was running through her head, Harriet studied Jasper dispassionately. He was so tall and although not broad, neither was he thin — more an athletic physique, which, all at once, she found dizzyingly attractive.

Invariably, ever-so slightly rumpled, reminding Harriet of the eccentric professors she met occasionally at museums, Jasper was not, never had been, considered a 'catch' by those who dictated such things, for he was not a slave to the latest foppish fashions, preferring more sober attire.

His dark brown hair barely skimmed his collar and his eyes… Harriet felt an odd flutter run through her as she lifted her gaze… she swore his arresting brown eyes could read her thoughts. She gulped and blushed but, although embarrassed by her wayward thoughts was unable to look away.

At the same time, Jasper was appraising Harriet. That yearning to kiss her freckled nose — currently crinkled in what should be a fierce, but was actually the most adorable, manner — skittered once more through his consciousness.

Emmeline whispered into his mind, reminding him Harriet had been the only one, outside his immediate family, to ignore requests to leave him alone after her death, refusing to let him become mired in grief. It was time to return the favour.

"How about we take one of those carriage rides, you insisted would be good for me all those years ago, then mayhap a short stroll?"

Where had that come from? Jasper wondered, astonished. *He had an appointment at White's, well, maybe not an appointment as such… no… this was lunacy. What on earth possessed him?*

Then he glanced at Harriet and knew even wild horses could not make him retract his offer.

Harriet and Joanna stared at him, then out of the window where snow blanketed the ground and a hard frost gripped the earth, eyebrows raised.

Jasper elaborated, "I think we need to do something completely unrelated to the waltz and, although 'tis cold, the fresh air will do us good."

Joanna jumped off the piano stool. "Yes let's. Come on, Harry, you know you love the park in winter, and at this time of day it will be quiet."

Harriet gave in for, in truth, she would appreciate a walk. She needed to clear her head of all the nonsense bouncing around.

Shortly thereafter, bundled up in their warm outdoor attire, the three were rattling along in the Rochford carriage, choosing to leave the top down, enjoying the chill air. They chattered in the effortless manner of friends, cheerful voices carrying in the stillness, and Harriet forgot to be grouchy.

Soon, they were in the tranquil surrounds of Hyde Park, their driver coming to a halt near one of the popular pathways.

Jasper helped both ladies down, and they sauntered slowly alongside the Serpentine. The waterway was frozen at the edges and the view, spectacular. A few ducks braved the frosty weather, sliding across the ice to where the water still flowed, their ungainly antics making the three watching laugh.

Pine, yew, and holly offered varying shades of green; a welcome splash of colour amongst the stark, silver, grey and white landscape. The ground crunched underfoot, and their breath hung on the air like misty cobwebs.

After a little while, Harriet ventured. "I apologise for my behaviour earlier, my lord. 'Twas unfair of me, alluding to your...

errr… you know…" she couldn't finish, unwilling to bring it up again.

Jasper smiled, and Harriet was certain her insides were turning to mush.

"'Tis of no matter, my lady. I daresay you are wearied of all the practicing. I do believe, if you continue with your endeavour, you will be fine come Friday. Moreover, your candour is refreshing. I recall you were never one to refrain from chastising me, when you felt it necessary." Chuckling at Harriet's response, which sounded something like *harrummpphh*.

They were diverted from what might have become an awkward topic by a shout from behind. All three turned and, to Harriet's astonishment, Joanna blushed bright pink.

"Joanna?" she queried.

Her friend shook her head and pressed her lips together, as a young gentleman on horseback approached. When he reached the trio, he slid off and bowed to the ladies who dipped neat curtseys, while nodding at Jasper.

"Lady Joanna. What a pleasant surprise. I was only thin—" he stopped abruptly, hectic red staining his cheeks.

Taking pity on him, Joanna said. "Fre… Lord Althorpe, you already know Lady Harriet, but may I present my brother, Lord Rochford?" Introductions made, Joanna launched into an animated discourse with the new arrival, leaving Jasper and Harriet standing somewhat uncomfortably to one side.

Jasper offered Harriet his arm. "Mayhap we could walk a little way along this path. Not so far as to cause questions, but I believe these two might appreciate a little privacy."

Harriet dithered, then acquiesced. Joanna didn't notice them leave, totally engrossed in her conversation.

"I had no idea Lord Frederick and she…" Harriet shook her head; stunned her best friend had kept this a secret. "Lord Frederick is partnered with Lady Sarah for the waltz. I never suspected a thing. I cannot recall Joanna even talking with him at rehearsal."

Harriet glanced over her shoulder, shaking her head again. "They look so..."

"In love?" supplied Jasper, perhaps a little cynically.

Harriet nodded, Joanna's sparkling eyes and pink cheeks evidence of how enamoured she was with the young gentleman.

Lord Frederick Althorpe, eldest son of the Marquis of Taverstock, was an affable fellow; rather shy and nothing like some of the rakes who stalked Society balls. Harriet realised her friend might well have found someone who yearned to be her partner for much longer than a five-minute waltz.

"I'm glad, she deserves someone who will adore her."

"What about you, Harriet? Do you not deserve the same?"

Harriet gave an unladylike snort of mirth. "I do not suppose anyone would love me so unconditionally," she demurred.

"I am too headstrong. The few who hinted they might like to ply their suit led me to understand, should they do so, and it became..." she hesitated, "...something serious, I would be expected to curb my ways. They were each dispatched with a flea in their ear."

She smiled, although Jasper saw little humour in it. "I refuse to wed someone who wishes to control me. I want to be loved for who I am, not what Society dictates a woman ought to be. I find most genteel pursuits irritatingly dull.

"I much prefer being outdoors in the fresh air, walking or riding, to sitting around a parlour gossiping. Where's the fun in that? Oh, the utter joy of being far away in the countryside, to enjoy the freedom to wander at will, without constraint."

She looked up at him. "I know 'tis a foolish dream, but I cling to it. 'Tis what keeps me from going mad when I am surrounded by simpering debutantes." Bending her head, embarrassed by her outburst.

Jasper stopped in the middle of the path and faced her. Unable to stop himself, he ran a gloved finger under her chin and tilted her head.

Their eyes met and, to Harriet, his gaze felt like a caress. Involuntarily, she leaned towards him as his voice wrapped around her.

"Never let go of your dream, Harriet Winterbourne, for should you allow another to snatch it away, you will become a mere shadow of yourself and that would be unconscionable."

The dark brown depths of his eyes seemed to touch her soul and although his finger scarcely brushed her skin, when his hand fell away, she felt bereft.

Chapter Four

A ll at once, Harriet wished Jasper would take her in his arms, the way he did when showing her the steps of the waltz.

No, not like that at all, she wanted more. She wanted to be held close, close enough to feel his body, to have his lips on hers. It flashed through her already befuddled mind that she wanted to dance with him, and only him, for the rest of her life.

A wish, Harriet knew to be preposterous, so, rather than dwell on what was not — what would never be — possible, she instilled a practical note into her voice and changed the subject.

"How about we sit here for a while?" Pointing to a convenient bench at the edge of the path. "We can see Joanna but not over-hear her conversation."

"As you please."

They sat for several minutes in companionable silence, admiring the scenery then, for no reason she could think of, Harriet asked softly, "Will you tell me about her?"

Jasper who was leaning back against the bench, legs outstretched, hands clasped over his stomach, shot upright and gaped at her.

"Beg pardon?" *Had he heard her correctly?*

She repeated her question, adding, "'Tis is as though Emmeline never existed. No one mentions her name, dare not draw attention to her accident for fear of upset. The lady I recall was fun loving and exuberant, unfailingly optimistic, and never without a smile.

"How could a person possessed of such vitality be... well... erased from everyone's minds as though she had never lived? Yet, so important, her death caused you to retreat from m... society." Catching herself before she said something she could not retract.

Harriet sounded genuinely interested, and Jasper who had never discussed Emmeline with anyone... not even his own family, conceded Harriet was right. No one ever talked about her. Maybe it was time.

As he hesitated, Harriet, not pausing to weigh her actions, laid her slender hand over his, squeezing his fingers gently. "Please Jasper. I do believe it might be time," unconsciously reiterating his thoughts.

Jasper studied their hands, then lifted his gaze to her face, seeing only warm encouragement. Her startlingly green eyes held his, pleading silently and, as was becoming a habit where Harriet was concerned, he heard himself start to speak.

"Emmeline was beautiful." He felt a slight flinch through Harriet's gloved fingers, and without thinking, rubbed his thumb over her knuckles. "Happy, bright, cheerful — all those things you just mentioned, but she was not all sweetness and light. She had a temper and was not afraid to offer an opinion on any topic, whether 'twas appropriate to do so or not."

He grinned in recollection of the arguments they used to have, describing the young lady whose life had been snatched away, so abruptly; his words helping Harriet to form a picture in her head.

Once he started, Jasper could not stop but, as he talked, it was a though a burden, one he did not realise he was carrying, was rolling off his shoulders. He had buried memories of Emmeline along with his heart, but he was still here, still breathing and, for the last few days, his heart no longer felt cold and empty.

Without trying, Harriet had somehow broken through, shattering his defences, and he felt more alive than he had in four years. Her glorious eyes and enchanting smile popped into his head at the most inopportune moments throughout the day and, at night, in his dreams — well least said about them the better.

He wrenched his attention back to Harriet who was listening intently her head cocked to one side. He felt his heartbeat rise and tightened his grip on her hand, gratified to feel her fingers curl around his.

"Thank you, Jasper. I feel not only do I know Emmeline, but also, I understand why you shied away from everyone. It would be difficult being expected, constantly, to answer questions about a love you had lost. Mayhap now you have spoken of her, she can rest."

Jasper frowned, it was such an odd thing to say, yet Emmeline had been circling the edge of his mind lately. Assuming it related to the time of year, Harriet's comment gave him pause. He did not believe in ghosts, but neither could he deny something inexplicable had prompted his words and behaviour.

Not prepared to speculate, he made do with a simple, "Perhaps."

Emmeline smiled. It was true, she was wearied of loitering in the shadows waiting for Jasper to let her go. She knew he had not been passionately in love with her, but his affection was all she needed. Had she not died in that stupid accident, they would have muddled along quite amicably.

That said, as she watched his face and sensed his emotions when he was near Harriet, Emmeline wondered whether she believed it. Perched on the back of the bench, observing them, she hoped they would acknowledge their feelings sooner rather than later. She couldn't wait around much longer.

Jasper and Harriet were still holding hands. Harriet did not want to let go, but knew she had to. Withdrawing her fingers, she stood, shaking out her skirts and drawing her cloak more closely around her shoulders. Despite the sunshine, the air remained chill.

"Brrrr… I think we should return to Joa—" at the same time as Jasper said,

"Harriet," in the most peculiar tone of voice, almost a sigh. He was standing right next to her and she angled her head, the better to look him in the eye. As he had done barely half an hour previously, Jasper stroked a finger along her jaw, the heat in his gaze stirring something utterly intoxicating deep within her soul.

She sucked in a breath and tried to speak but her voice was husky, and words refused to form.

"J-Jasper?" she croaked, finally, reaching out to him, only to let her hand fall.

Don't be foolish, she admonished herself. *You are reading more into this than is there. Jasper isn't interested in you romantically. No doubt he considers you too young and far too silly. He is simply grateful for a sympathetic ear. He is doing a favour for his sister.*

She hiccuped on an unexpected sob. *Grow up, Harriet.*

Disconcerted by her thoughts, Harriet could not remain so close, unable to face him, for surely, she had mis-read his smouldering expression. She forced herself to move, walking away from the path, towards the water's edge, needing to gather her chaotic thoughts.

Jasper, suffering a similar confusion, watched the myriad of emotions chase across her face, and was puzzled when she turned and walked away.

"Harriet," he called.

Ignoring him, with head bent and shoulders hunched, she scuffed through the leaves along the riverbank.

"Harriet be careful, the…" he never finished his warning.

At the same moment, Harriet stepped heavily on what she presumed to be solid ground but which was, in fact, the layer of ice at the water's edge, camouflaged by moss and reeds. It wasn't thick enough to bear any weight and she pitched sideways.

Arms cartwheeling, desperately trying to balance herself, Harriet heard her mother's voice, as though she was there on the footpath.

Harriet Winterbourne you **thoughtless** *girl! What possessed you to walk along the riverbank? You might know this would happen.*

One day her mother might be proud of her, but it certainly would not be today, *and now Jasper will see you for the ungainly ninny you are,* she chastised herself. *Just great!*

There was an almighty splash when Harriet hit the water. It wasn't very deep, but her heavy cloak pulled her under. The water was frigid, causing her to gasp in shock, gulping down half the river — or so it seemed — in the process. She flailed her arms trying to get her head above the water, but it was too hard, and she felt herself sinking.

Panicking, she opened her mouth to scream, swallowing even more water, as various waterfowl — their quiet foraging rudely interrupted — rose into the sky in an outraged flap of wings and, with raucous cries, circled above them before coming back to roost further up the Serpentine.

The three remaining on dry land ran towards the bank — of Harriet there was no sign.

"*Harriet*," Joanna shrieked, as Frederick and Jasper waded into the icy river, searching for her, frantically.

After what felt like far too long, but was barely a minute...
"Got her," grunted Jasper. "Here, Althorpe, give me a hand."

The two men hauled the sodden woman out of the water. Her lips were an unhealthy shade of blue and she appeared to be unconscious. Jasper laid her on the bank and called for Joanna.

"Joanna, I want you to place your hand over her heart." Joanna did as he asked, sliding her hand under the wet cloak and against Harriet's chest. "Does it beat?"

Each held their breath, with Joanna willing the throb of a heartbeat to pulse against her hand.

Precious seconds ticked by, then she nodded.

"Yes, it is beating."

Relief poured through them, as they watched Jasper press down hard on Harriet's chest. Once, twice, then she lurched upright, liquid spewing from her mouth as her lungs expelled the deadly water.

She coughed, retching helplessly.

Frederick ran to the carriage, urging the driver along the track. By the time the carriage reached the group, Harriet was conscious, but shivering, and feeling like an utter idiot.

"S-sorry, s-so s-sorry," she stammered.

"Hush, sweetheart," Jasper soothed. "See the carriage is here we'll have you home in a jiffy."

Harriet heard the endearment, but was too cold to register its import, all her concentration on trying to get warm, aware of being lifted, and of a hurried discussion about the doctor and where to send him.

She tried to tell them to take her home, but Jasper hushed her again.

"Chesterfield Street is closer than Harewood Place. I will send someone to inform your family once we have you safely there."

Chapter Five

Harriet never recalled the next little while with any clarity.

She had no idea, she was bundled into several thick rugs, or that someone rubbed her arms continually, in an effort to keep her circulation from becoming sluggish. That her head lolled onto Jasper's shoulder, and that she muttered about how comfortable it felt.

Nor did anyone enlighten her.

Lord Frederick rode ahead, first to call for the doctor, then on to Rochford House to warn them of the impending arrival of a very wet Lady Harriet.

By the time the carriage rolled up, everyone had sprung into action. A hot bath was already drawn with plenty of towels gathered. A warming pan had been slipped between the sheets in one of the guest bedchambers, and hot sweet tea was brewing on the stove.

Jasper refused to relinquish his hold until they were upstairs, and, even then, it took all Joanna's powers of persuasion to get him to allow their staff to take over.

Reluctantly, he sat Harriet in one of the chairs, whereupon the maids fussed around her, but had to be dragged from the room by his sister.

"You cannot be in the room while they remove her clothes, Jasper. What are you thinking?" she chided. "Harry will be fine. You rescued her quickly, and we were home within fifteen minutes."

Jasper knew Joanna was right, which did not stop him worrying. For a brief moment when he hauled Harriet out of the river, he thought she had died. To lose one love was bad enough, to lose another... *wait... love?*

No, he was not in love. He couldn't be. He barely knew Harriet.

Ahh, but of course you do, his heart reminded. *Harriet has been in your life almost since her birth. Joanna and she have been inseparable for years. If you think about it, you know everything about her. You know what makes her laugh, causes her pain, brings that joyful smile to her lips, or draws shadows across her face.*

'Tis likely you have been in love with her longer than you realise, only you refused to recognise it. You think her too good for you. Well perhaps you ought to ask Harriet what she *thinks.*

Jasper closed his mind to the uproar in his head, and turned his concentration to pacing the floor. Doctor Hardy, the Ogilvie's physician, arrived and was escorted upstairs. He took his time, causing Jasper's anxiety to become dread, for it seemed an age until he reappeared.

Informing those waiting — less than patiently — Harriet had not come to any lasting harm, more chilled than anything, the doctor praised the two gentlemen for their speedy response to her tumble.

Both men acknowledged the accolade, then Frederick took his leave, saying he would expect an update later, at practice.

Joanna walked with him to the front door, returning to the parlour with a dreamy look on her face. One, upon which, she was thankful, no one commented.

"You may go and see her if you like." Dr Hardy waved his hand absently in the direction of the guest room, as Lady Rochford invited him to partake of a cup of hot chocolate in the parlour.

Jasper took the stairs two a time, startling Joanna who was still perplexed by his behaviour.

Following more sedately, when she entered the room, light dawned. Jasper was sitting by the bed, holding Harriet's hand and stroking it. Ignoring the rather inappropriate conduct of her brother, Joanna hugged herself in glee, seeing quite clearly what neither Jasper nor Harriet were prepared to admit. It would please her immensely to see her friend and brother wed.

Harriet, while relishing the gentle touch of Jasper's fingers, was mortified, her cheeks flushed. She certainly knew how to ruin a lovely walk, but her apology was brushed aside.

"It was an accident. I'm sure you did not mean to frighten the ducks or drink half the river. Good job 'tis the middle of winter — people will not be able to punt along it for weeks after the amount you swallowed, fair drank it dry you did." Jasper dropped a slow wink, making Harriet blush even more, though this time with uncharacteristic shyness.

"Are you warm enough?" Joanna interposed.

"Yes, thank you. Please, I am sorry to inconvenience your family like this. It was my own stupid fault. Apparently, I am incapable of putting one foot in front of the other, even on the edge of a river. Oh, and what about practice? I cannot miss any more."

Harriet threw back the covers and made to get out of bed, unaware the fine cotton of the borrowed nightgown left little to the imagination, prompting Jasper to bite down on groan at the sight of her lissom figure.

"Get back into bed, Harriet Winterbourne," a booming voice instructed from the doorway, and Lady Conway swept into the room.

Harriet's face crumpled, *now she was in for it.*

Jasper watched in fascination as she reverted to childhood in front of his eyes. He had never known anyone to cow Harriet, not entirely sure, he approved.

Standing, he bowed. "Good afternoon Lady Conway. I trust you are well?"

"Yes, yes... young Jasper isn't it?" Lady Conway peered at the grave faced gentleman, who had been sitting by the bed, in which her daughter was currently ensconced. She sensed undercurrents but, blessed with little imagination, was unable to discern what they were.

Shaking her head at such sentimentality, she continued, imperiously, "Yes, I am fine. Fortunately, despite hearing my daughter has hurled herself into the Serpentine on a winter's afternoon, which ought to give her poor mother the vapours, I have a strong constitution." Brushing passed him, she went over to the bed.

Jasper, torn between wanting to stay with Harriet, and removing himself from her mother's gimlet gaze, asked whether Lady Conway would like a cup of hot coffee or perhaps tea.

"Thank you, young man, a cup of tea would be much appreciated. 'Tis bitter out there and I wager it will snow again before the day's over."

Hiding a smile at being referred to as 'young' twice in less than five minutes, Jasper disappeared, intent on organising refreshments. As he headed to the stairs, Lady Conway's strident tones reverberated along the hall.

"Now then my girl, what were you thinking? You must learn to behave with poise. You will never attract a husband with your clumsiness. Unmarriageable, that's what you are. Honestly you will be the death of me," she scolded her daughter.

Whatever else she had to say was rendered indistinguishable when the door swung closed, but Jasper's heart clenched at Lady Conway's words, imaging Harriet's face as she was berated.

Did her mother really think Harriet unmarriageable? The thought of her marrying one of the eligible bachelors currently on the hunt for a wealthy bride, sent a disagreeable jolt all the way through him.

He could not let that happen. They wouldn't love her, care for her, cherish her in the same way he wanted to... yet again, his thoughts tumbled into disarray.

The way he *wanted to. Well dammit, this was a pretty pickle. What was he going to do about it?*

Realising, right there and then, he could do nothing, Jasper pushed it aside to focus on what he *was* able to do, and rang for tea.

Another hour slid by before Jasper ventured back upstairs to the guest room. Lady Conway had just left, thanking Lady Rochford for her generosity, and affirming she would send a coach the following day to collect Harriet.

The house seemed to breathe a sigh of relief at her departure, relaxing back into its natural state of refined informality.

Joanna had remained with Harriet, refusing to abandon her to the tender mercies of her mother; her presence ensuring Lady Conway at least tempered her irritation towards her only daughter.

Jasper knocked quietly and was admitted by his sister, who placed a finger to her lips.

"Harriet's asleep. Best not disturb her, the doctor said she should rest. She has warmed up, finally, and has drunk some of Mabel's tea," referring to a beverage their cook concocted, guaranteed to cure all ailments.

Jasper chuckled and, although would have preferred to sit with Harriet, if only to watch her sleep, bowed to propriety and accompanied Joanna to the dining room where they partook of a very late luncheon.

"I must go to practise. Lady Hereford will get herself in a flap if two of us fail to attend. Freddie... err... Lord Althorpe, said he would collect me," a becoming pink, painting her cheeks once again, when Jasper raised a quizzical brow. "Fret not, I will have Rosa accompany me." Joanna reassured — Rosa being her maid and sometime chaperone.

"Do I need to speak with this Lord Freddie?"

Joanna shook her head "Not yet... maybe... I wish... too soon..." she trailed off uncertainly.

Jasper grinned at her discomfiture. "From what I observed today, he appears personable, and I know of his family."

Joanna narrowed her eyes, watchfully.

Jasper shrugged. "I may have been out of circulation for a while, but that does not mean I am wholly unaware of what goes on around me."

His sister tried to appear nonchalant, but Jasper was not fooled — she was enamoured of this Lord Frederick. From what he gathered, she could do worse, but made a mental note to have a quiet conversation with young Althorpe when next the opportunity presented itself. In the meantime, there was still this wretched dance.

It was late afternoon before Harriet woke, momentarily disoriented in the unfamiliar surrounds. Then everything flooded back. Falling in the Serpentine, a doctor examining her, her mother breathing fire.

Oh her mother, honestly — Harriet was starting to wonder whether her mother would ever smile at her. She could not remember the last time such an earth-shattering event occurred.

Then there was Jasper... what had Jasper done? She creased her brow, a vague recollection of him calling her sweetheart and holding her hand, flittering through her consciousness. Harriet knew that could not be right, but the memory lingered; the touch of his hand, the light stroke of his fingers.

Mayhap it was a dream, the mere idea enough to send turbulent heat spiralling through her. *No Harry, don't even think it, he is Joanna's brother and perhaps a friend. He was just looking out for you — nothing more than that.* All rational arguments aside, she yearned to feel his hand on hers again, if only to prove she was not imagining things.

What if... Harriet closed her mind, refusing to accept even the remotest possibility. Jasper was besotted with Emmeline, likely he would be for the rest of his life.

As she contemplated this, her brow still furrowed and her countenance dark, Harriet had the most extraordinary impression there was someone in the room with her. She glanced around but could see no one.

Despite a day turned gloomy — the predicted snow already falling — the room was well lit. Curtains were tied back, a fire crackled in the grate, and there were several candelabra scattered around.

Nowhere for anyone to hide.

"Who's there?" No response. "Silly girl, Harry," she chided. "Now you're talking to yourself. Being half-drowned has clouded your senses." She grinned at her own nonsense, when something made her pause.

"Do not lose faith Harriet, he will find you. He just needs a push." The words drifted through Harriet's mind.

"Errr... hmmm... pardon me?" A twinge of unease prickled down her spine. The voice repeated the words, then silence.

Harriet gulped, clutching the bed clothes, more unnerved than she would ever admit, pinching herself just to be sure she was still awake.

Then it came again,

"'Tis you who will rescue his heart."

All Harriet could think was, she must be coming down with a chill, and was currently in the throes of a fever-induced dream — but as the voice continued to echo softly, like the dying notes of a harp, it came to her.

Could it be?

Emmeline!

Chapter Six

Two days later, Harriet presented herself at Rochford House, none the worse for her unintentional dip in the river or her possible encounter with a ghost. Although her acute embarrassment at the ensuing fuss lingered, she had stopped apologising to all and sundry at every opportunity.

Joanna insisted they continue with her lessons as there were only three days left until the ball, and it was better to keep practising until the last minute.

Lady Hereford had pronounced herself satisfied with Harriet's efforts and, despite that young lady's pleas the previous day, absolutely refused to grant her permission to withdraw.

"Lady Harriet, when I say I want ten couples that is precisely what I want, not nine not eleven. Goodness me, where is the backbone to match that red hair of yours," her trenchant tones brooking no argument

That did the trick. Harriet gathered her failing confidence around her and applied herself, wholeheartedly, to the dance. Her partner, Lord Roger Pelham, was, in her opinion, a bit of a fop; more concerned with keeping up with the racy crowd he was part of, than participating in the gentlemanly pursuits of the other bachelors chosen for the performance.

This *did* mean, he was not on the hunt for a bride. Moreover, he was quite a comical fellow, able to induce a fit of the giggles with irrepressible frequency, effectively diverting her when she missed a step or tripped over her own feet, for which she could forgive him any number of faults.

When she arrived at the Ogilvie residence that morning, Harriet was feeling more hopeful than she had since this debacle was first proposed. Joanna let her in, and the two began gossiping about Lord Freddie, who had asked Joanna to accompany him to Lord Beaumont's New Year's Ball.

A glittering occasion attended by everyone who was anyone and second only in importance to the Hereford's Christmas Eve Ball. The promise of a new year seemed to encourage courtships between those normally too reticent to approach the girl of their — or their parents' — dreams, and Joanna was hoping, this year, Freddie might be one of them.

Several moments later, this was how Jasper came upon them when he strolled into the room. Harriet was curled up on the chaise under the window, her flaming hair unravelling from its neat bun, her lovely green eyes brimming with amusement at whatever she and Joanna were nattering about. He paused in the doorway, observing her through hooded eyes.

To his surprise, Jasper found he missed Harriet when the Conway carriage whisked her away. Allowed out of bed, the evening of her dunking, Harriet had proved to be a congenial dinner guest.

Lifelong friends with the whole of his family, she was relaxed in their company and, never one to stay quiet when subjects dear to her heart were being discussed, launched into a heated exchange with Edward, his younger brother, regarding one of the current social problems.

Watching them debate, Jasper was impressed with Harriet's grasp and understanding of the situation, and her refusal to be intimidated by Edward's pompous attitude.

Her animated features while she talked, her expressive hands emphasising her point, caused his heart to trip. Not for the first time, since she had whirled back into his life, he wished there was no one else around, so he could kiss her senseless.

Every moment in her company added to Jasper's growing awareness that Harriet was everything he didn't think he wanted, yet now craved. A beautiful, spirited young woman who was his intellectual equal and who would doubtless challenge and thwart him at every turn.

Life with her would be lively, entertaining, stimulating, invigorating but never, *ever* dull. Then common sense reasserted itself, along with the notion, she probably thought of him in the same light, she did Edward — a rather irritating, older brother — deliberately ignoring the ache such a realisation engendered.

Now, she was here again, and he steeled himself to remain unruffled by her presence. Shrugging rational impartiality over him like a dinner jacket, he stepped forward.

"Good morning, Lady Harriet." He bowed as Harriet slid off the chaise and curtseyed. "I trust you are suffering no ill effects from your antics in the river?" He summoned up a grin.

Harriet rolled her eyes. "According to Mama, I should be very thankful my, and I quote 'giddy tomfoolery,' was not witnessed by any of her friends. Her humiliation in having so graceless a daughter, might have caused her to retreat to Winterbourne Manor for the remainder of the winter."

She spoke pertly and with no little humour, but Jasper discerned a resigned sadness lurking in her eyes. That Lady Conway cared more for her own reputation than the well-being of her only daughter, while apparently not unusual, evidently still had the power to wound.

Willing her to smile again, Jasper, instead of commenting on this, sought to divert, "Let us not dwell on such matters and apply ourselves to the dance. Three days until your grand performance. Joanna?" His sister went over to the piano. "Today we are going to add a flourish, but…" chuckling at Harriet's horrified expression, "…let us refresh our memory with what you have already learned."

As the lilting melody filled the room, the two took their positions on the polished floor — the rug already rolled up out of the way. Jasper placed his right hand on Harriet's waist, his left hand grasping her right hand.

Harriet, hesitating for a split second, lifted her left hand to his right shoulder and began counting the beat of the music. Before she knew it, they were moving through the steps of the waltz, to a pattern and rhythm now ingrained in her head.

Jasper was captivated by the way Harriet's lips moved as she counted the beats soundlessly, eyes closed, her adorable nose, once again, crinkled in concentration, and it took everything in him not to kiss the tip.

Distracting himself, he signalled to Joanna who paused in her playing. Harriet stepped out of his arms and tilted her head, waiting.

"You are now proficient enough for the performance on Friday, but I think we should add one or two more turns, so you are familiar with most of the combinations."

Harriet heaved a dramatic sigh. "On your own head, or feet be it," she cautioned. "You should be grateful, I have conquered these steps, to add more complicated moves merely confirms you are either addled or have greater faith in my abilities than sense dictates." She contorted her face into the most appalling grimace, drawing a burst of laughter from the siblings.

"I am neither addled nor insensible," Jasper replied his face creased with amusement. "You will be the belle of this ball, otherwise my competence as a teacher is woefully lacking. Come…" he stepped forward, and Harriet lifted her chin, slipping her hand into his, a frisson from even so slight a touch trickling along her arm.

To Harriet's chagrin, Joanna, at a word from her brother, started playing a different waltz. Glaring at her partner, Harriet fumbled as she strove to adjust to the change in music, noting with some asperity, Jasper was not in the least perturbed.

He simply leaned closer, murmuring, "Stop over thinking it and let your body go with the music. When dancing the waltz, it should appear as though you are floating, not tramping through a swamp."

Harriet giggled at the image that evoked and completely lost her place, tripping over Jasper's left foot.

She landed against him and, without thinking, he wrapped his arm around her. She could feel the erratic beat of his heart and her breathing quickened. All at once she wished they were alone, far away, where convention did not apply, and she might be so bold as to kiss him.

"I… errr… so sorry," she muttered, righting herself, her face bright pink from such brazen desires.

"It is of no matter, shall we continue?" Came the smooth reply, prompting Harriet to suppose she had imagined it. Nodding, she resumed her place and the rest of the time went by without a hiccup.

Too soon, or so it felt to Harriet, their half hour was over but, rather than leave, Jasper asked whether the two ladies fancied a short constitutional before luncheon.

No more snow had fallen, and the pathways were swept. The

day, although cold, was bright and sunny, and a walk did sound inviting. Moments later they were sauntering along the path towards Berkley Square.

Despite the unfashionable hour they were not the only ones abroad; the rattle of carriages, clip-clop of horses' hooves and chatter of people — bright sounds on the gentle breeze. The three talked about upcoming festivities, arriving back at Rochford House, invigorated.

Jasper excused himself after luncheon, claiming a business meeting, yet Harriet could not shake the curious feeling it was her presence in which he was uncomfortable. She was at a loss as to why, but that it might be, made her heart ache.

Determined he would never know of her idiotic *tendre*, she forced all the gentle hints and ghostly assurances out of her mind, and became the Harriet Winterbourne everyone else expected her to be; practical, accomplished and totally uninterested in love.

Emmeline scrunched up her face in exasperation. *No!* **No!** **No!** *This would not do. Honestly, youngsters these days needed their heads banging together. The dance was almost upon them; there was no time to dillydally with love.*

Thursday morning saw Harriet arrive for her penultimate rehearsal. She was beginning to feel nervous. Papa had informed her that everyone who was anyone would be attending the ball, and Mama took pains to remind Harriet just what was at stake if she messed up the performance.

Harriet knew she was capable. She had mastered the steps, the turns, the rise and the fall, and could even manage a flourish. In fact, so impressed was Lady Hereford that, at one point during last afternoon's session, she had actually smiled and said how gracefully she... yes, she... Harriet, moved around the floor. It did seem as though their tireless efforts had paid off, perhaps this performance might be a cause for gossip long after the party.

It would be, but for reasons none could possibly imagine.

Chapter Seven

Their usual half an hour lengthened into an hour, the time disappearing in the blink of an eye. The two dancing came to a graceful standstill, panting slightly from their exertions, and Jasper pronounced himself pleased with Harriet's achievement.

She grinned at his praise, commenting at least his beleaguered feet would no longer have to suffer from her incautious steps.

"I daresay they will recover given time." He chuckled.

Aware she was still in his arms, Harriet blushed and, as she stepped away, a chill breeze cut between them. Odd, where did that come from? She looked around, presuming the door had swung open, but it remained closed and, until that moment, the room had been overly warm.

Shrugging it off, she moved closer to the hearth.

Joanna rang for coffee, then saying she would be back shortly, dashed out.

"Joanna never walks anywhere does she?" Harriet smiled, hearing her footsteps pounding up the stairs, wincing when a loud bang all but rattled the house.

Jasper shook his head in amused resignation, joining her by the fire.

A tranquillity settled over the room, and Harriet was intensely aware of Jasper who was barely a step away from her.

About to say something, anything, to keep the congenial atmosphere from becoming strained, she was shoved towards him by what felt like a hand.

Jasper, desperately trying to come up with an innocuous topic of conversation was startled when Harriet seemed to stumble. On what he could not fathom, but in light of the last couple of weeks it would not surprise him if she tripped over air.

Instinctively, he put a hand out to steady her as she fell against him.

"B-beg pardon," she stammered, frowning, not quite sure what was going on. "That was peculiar, almost as though someone pushed me."

Glancing over her shoulder, she recalled that eerie moment in the guest bedroom. Facing Jasper who still had his hand on her arm, one eyebrow raised quizzically, she blushed, uncharacteristically shy.

"Pay me no mind it's only, when I was here the other day, I thought I heard…" She clamped her lips together. *Really Harriet? Tell him you think you heard the voice of his lost love? He'll think all that river water you consumed has disturbed your mind.*

Jasper didn't answer. His brain badgered him to reply, but words stuck in his throat, as he was held in thrall by her beautiful eyes, his desire to kiss her nose almost overwhelming. Etiquette decreed he stop this madness but, he had not the will.

Seconds ticked by.

Harriet could not tear away her gaze and, despite knowing what she was about to do was inexcusable, the whole of the King's cavalry could not have prevented her.

"My lord, thank you for your kindness and your patience. I should still be fumbling blindly through the waltz if not for you. Please believe me when I say, my grouchy moments aside, I have truly enjoyed these sessions and I hope you will forgive me."

"Forgive you? Why would I need to forgive you?" his tones baffled.

"For my shameless behaviour." She smiled up at him, admiring his, typically, slightly dishevelled appearance. His cravat was askew, his shirt was coming untucked, and his waistcoat, unbuttoned. A tremor ran through her, aware she might easily ruin their friendship, but she had to risk it.

"Shameless beh—" His words were cut off as Harriet, taking her courage in both hands, stretched up on her toes and brushed her lips against his. "Harriet…" he rasped, searching her face.

The fire in her cheeks almost matched that of her hair, but her eyes were wary.

"Harriet," he repeated, then groaning, threw caution to the winds and returned her kiss, with a fervour, which should have shocked but instead felt as natural as breathing.

Had the pair registered anything else around them, they might have been forgiven for thinking the room glowed more brightly in one corner, as Emmeline's ethereal face lit up in a satisfied smile.

Thank goodness for that, surely now my task is complete.

Jasper's head was whirling. What was he thinking, here in the middle of the parlour where anyone could happen upon them? He was placing Harriet in an untenable position, if they were caught. Yet he was falling deeper and deeper into their kiss.

She felt so perfect in his embrace, her willowy figure clung to his lean frame as though specifically designed to do so. He trailed one hand up her back, into her lustrous hair, fingers entangling in the silky locks, while his other splayed around her waist, holding her as close as he dared, feeling the chaotic thrum of her heart, mirroring that of his own.

Harriet, meantime was matching him kiss for kiss, her head upbraiding her for such audacity, her heart delighting in the wanton deliciousness. The longer he kissed her, the more she knew — Jasper Ogilvie, Lord Rochford was the only man she would ever love. Eager fingers sought and found the spot where his shirt was loose, stroking over heated skin, and she was gratified to hear him catch his breath.

Just as Harriet wondered whether she was delirious with the ardour flaring through her, Jasper broke their kiss, but continued to hold her, pillowing his cheek on her head while he tried to steady his breathing.

"Harriet Winterbourne never have I ever..." he stopped, unsure quite what he should say.

Harriet, although loath to break contact, wriggled out of his arms and sank a neat curtsy. "Neither have I, but I'm glad I did."

Her cheeky wink and impish smile, tugged a chuckle from Jasper, diffusing heightened emotions.

Harriet cocked her head and studied him for a moment; her hand, trembling slightly, rose to cup his cheek, cool fingers tracing his jawline. "I am so very glad I did."

Jasper bent his head and did what he wanted to do since first they danced — he kissed her nose. Then, knowing Joanna would likely burst through the door at any moment, moved away and leaned against the mantel.

"Jasper, would you, that is I hoped... if possible... mayhap..." Harriet ground to a halt, twiddling her fingers together.

Emmeline, figuratively, held her breath, as Harriet sucked in a large one of her own.

"Might you come tomorrow evening? I do believe to dance with you at the ball would be marvellous, after... well... you know..." even though she had just flouted every convention, Harriet still couldn't bring herself to say what she meant, what she really wanted — it was not done. This way she opened the door but not so wide, a draught couldn't swing it closed.

Jasper wanted nothing more than to hold Harriet in his arms for the rest of his life but, at the Hereford's Ball? The one occasion he had no intention of attending. The entire *ton* would be there, it was the event of the winter Season, yet his invitation remained unopened on his desk.

Everyone would be watching, muttering and, given it would be his first appearance at any ball since Emmeline's death, the gossips would have a field day. Not only was he uncertain he was ready for such scrutiny but also, he had no mind to subject Harriet to uncharitable prattle. It was enough her mother found fault with everything she did.

"Regretfully, I shall not attend. Mayhap next year," his abrupt response, not as prudent as it ought to have been.

Harriet's brow lowered.

Really? He could kiss her like that, yet not care enough to go to a stupid ball? One in which she *had not wanted to perform, in the first place, but allowed him to persuade her? Was he embarrassed at the thought of dancing with her in public?*

She wanted to cry but, instead, her fiery temper, the one she was rarely able to control, began to bubble. Before she could curb her tongue, her distress spilled over.

"So, my efforts during these last two weeks are not worthy of you, is that it? You have no qualms dancing with me here, with no witnesses, but the idea of actually being seen with me in a ballroom, in front of Society is simply too, *too* embarrassing. Not clumsy Lady Harriet, the one with two left feet."

Jasper tried to interrupt.

She ignored him, pacing the room in a fine old tantrum.

"Not only that, you kiss me as though I was the only woman in the world. Yes, I initiated it, but you kissed me until my legs turned to jelly and my brain to liquid. I suppose that is another thing you prefer to remain within this room? Duly noted."

She flicked her hand in dismissal. "I thought we were beginning to share something special. I thought, I hoped, you might feel for me, something akin to what I feel for you. I was not the one calling you, 'sweetheart.' Never fear, I will make no mention of it. Who would believe me anyway? Mayhap one day, some hapless and unsuspecting bachelor might fall under my feeble spell, for apparently any magic I might have is totally wasted on you. I pray the poor man has sturdy boots."

With this weak attempt at humour, Harriet dragged her cloak around her shoulders. "Please extend my apologies to Joanna, and tell her I shall see her this afternoon. You have made your position clear. I shall waste no more of your valuable time. Strange though…"

She paused, holding his gaze, all vivacity draining from her face. "…I thought you courageous, sincere, and honourable."

Without qualifying her remark, Harriet stormed out, flaming hair streaming behind her. She fled through the front door and down the steps to her waiting carriage, before Jasper could stop her.

Shortly thereafter, Joanna returned. She had been waylaid by their mother about some problem with her gown for the following evening, their discussion taking rather longer than anticipated.

"Where's Harry?" she asked, in bemusement, scanning the room as though expecting her friend to pop out from behind a chair.

"She had to leave. She said she would see you this afternoon." Jasper's face was like thunder and he stalked along to his study, slamming the door.

Joanna, not known for her tact, for once left well alone, determined to wheedle it out of Harriet later.

Emmeline huffed an aggrieved sigh. *Well that was just great! Now what was she going to do?*

Chapter Eight

Harriet was not at all forthcoming about whatever had happened in the parlour, when Joanna broached the topic that afternoon.

"Please leave it Joanna. Suffice it to say, once again I made a cake of myself. My mother is correct, I am a lost cause," Harriet spoke in a voice quite unlike her own and was all she would say.

Joanna was not fooled, not for a second, recalling the scene in the bedchamber when Jasper held Harriet's hand. Fleeting the moment may have been, but the depth of emotion in their expressions was not.

Joanna experienced a flash of anger towards Jasper. This was typical of her obdurate brother, just when she thought he was becoming more sociable, that he was beginning to live again, he goes and ruins the best thing that ever happened to him.

She ruminated over what to do throughout practice, and was so distracted, Lady Hereford felt obliged to remark upon it, to little effect it must be admitted.

. . .

The hours of practise coming to the fore, Harriet applied herself to the session, but it was as though someone had snuffed out a candle. She went through the motions, executing the steps with no small amount of grace, but she did not smile, she could not smile.

All the enjoyment connected to this dance because of being taught by Jasper had evaporated, and she did not care if she never smiled again.

The next day, Harriet sent her regrets to Rochford House, deeming it pointless. She had no desire to see Jasper who doubtless, would mollify her with platitudes, making the whole debacle even more humiliating.

Instead, she spent the morning ensuring her Christmas presents were organised, toys or books for her nephews and nieces, and thoughtful gifts for the staff.

On impulse, Harriet had purchased a token for Jasper, partly in thanks for giving up his time, and partly for saving her from drowning. She found it when browsing her favourite bookshop — it was not a new volume, bearing a wonderfully aged look — Shakespeare's *Taming of the Shrew*.

She thought it ironically appropriate, and assumed he would appreciate the humour behind her choice. Now, as she sat on her bed stroking her fingers over the burnished leather cover, it seemed irrelevant and a trifle absurd.

Sighing with the futility of it all, Harriet wrote a few heartfelt words on the flyleaf, then placed the book in the box she had purchased especially, tied a broad, dark green ribbon around it, and set it aside.

She intended to ask Joanna whether she would be kind enough to give it to Jasper the next morning — Christmas Day.

Once satisfied all her tasks were complete, she turned her attention to preparing for the ball.

Indulging in a long soak in a warm bath infused with a delicate fragrance, went a long way to soothing her fraught nerves. Her hair washed, Harriet sat by the fire while Annie, her maid, rubbed the heavy locks dry.

Inevitably, while she watched the flames cavorting in the hearth, her thoughts strayed to Jasper. His grave demeanour, softened by his tender smile, his rangy physique, his large yet gentle hands; all refused to be ignored, interposing themselves in her head most insistently — it really was utterly vexing.

In the quiet of her room, Harriet allowed herself the luxury, just for a moment, of imagining what might have been, when she made the idiotic mistake of believing in magic.

As the evening drew in, a stream of carriages rolled to a halt outside a stately residence in Grosvenor Square, where a multitude of windows glowed from the light of, what must have been, thousands of candles.

Strains of music could be heard through the imposing front doors, currently standing open as those arriving to provide the entertainment, hurried in, escaping the freezing air.

It wasn't snowing, but the weatherise predicted another fall before the night was out. Christmas would be white this year.

Harriet, huddled in a heavy cloak, hood covering her hair, stepped down from her carriage and climbed the steps, slowly, stopping to greet Mr Spencer the Hereford's butler, before passing through the doors.

Admiring the festive decorations, she wandered across the elegant entrance hall and down a shadowy corridor leading to the rooms the ladies would use to dress — their gowns hanging ready.

Lady Hereford had decided those in the performance should look as though they were at a masked ball and would be in two sets of five couples.

Eschewing the fashionable pale, and to her mind insipid, hues, the duchess had declared the gowns would resemble gemstones — emerald, ruby, citrine, sapphire and turquoise.

The men would wear traditional attire — silver grey pants and charcoal grey tailcoats, but their cravats and waistcoats matched the colour of their partner's gown.

The vibrant tones were repeated in the ornate masks, fashioned to allow the audience only a glimpse of the dancers' faces, without restricting the wearer's vision. Although rather fiddly to affix, even the men were won over by the clever design.

There was an air of suppressed excitement as the moment approached. Muffled laughter and snatches of light-hearted banter could be heard along the dim corridors as last minute preparations were undertaken.

Joanna was on her way to see whether she might sneak a few minutes with Freddy, when she overheard Lady Hereford's brusque tones.

"Damn the boy! What was he thinking? 'Tis a good job he sent a messenger for, had I got hold of him, I would box his ears. We have less than two hours, no time to find a replacement. Oh, this waltz will be the death of me."

Plenty of tut tutting ensued, prompting Joanna to change direction and follow the voices, which sounded as though they were heading to the ballroom.

"Your Grace," she called as she reached the duchess and Lady

Marchland — Lady Hereford's closest friend and sometime assistant for these gala events.

Lady Hereford spun around, her expression quizzical. "What is it? Why aren't you ready? Honestly," in an aside for Lady Marchland, "these girls, heads in the clouds, flibbertigibbets one and all."

She swung her steely gaze back to Joanna. "Now, what is it?"

"I do not mean to pry, Lady Hereford, but is one of the gentlemen unwell?"

"Unfortunately, that whelp Pelham is indisposed—"

"Pelham? Not Lord Roger?" Joanna interrupted without thinking, then remembered her manners and quickly dipped a curtsy. "Beg pardon, my lady." Her face bright red.

Lady Hereford looked down her aristocratic nose for a long moment until Joanna squirmed uncomfortably. "No matter. Yes — Lord Roger."

"Oh no, Harriet already thinks this performance is cursed. Now she will know 'tis true," Joanna wailed, but the moment the words left her mouth, a tantalising idea manifested itself. The small parcel Harriet had slipped her earlier, adding to her conviction. "Your Grace, I do believe I may be able to help."

Lady Hereford arched an eyebrow, and Joanna made her suggestion.

The duchess took less than two minutes to come to a decision. "I think it is the answer to our prayers, my dear."

"Jasper has suitable trousers and tailcoat but what about the waistcoat and cravat?" Joanna worried.

"Both are here, we had the men leave their garments in one of the guest chambers, I had no mind any would forget to bring them. Thank goodness Pelham is tall," she paused. "Will you persuade him?"

"Assuredly my lady, I know just what to say." Joanna gave the duchess a sly grin and shot off to grab her cloak.

"My, my, youngsters of today, so confidant, not like us. We

were angels in comparison." Lady Hereford nudged her friend, who merely held her gaze, until the duchess blushed — an unheard of occurrence — before nodding and walking away.

Lady Hereford chuckled, her madcap youth was something of a legend amongst her peers, but she preferred this bunch never found out. Smiling at the memory, she made her way to the rooms where the ladies were changing, feeling less anxious than she had ten minutes previously.

Harriet, who had heard about Lord Roger's shenanigans, was muttering angrily about cursed waltzes and imbecile partners. Her tirade, interrupted when Lady Hereford popped her head around the door to inform her, a gentleman had been prevailed upon to take Roger's place.

Startled, Harriet's jaw dropped. Who on earth had they managed to find at such short notice who knew this waltz?

The duchess did not see fit to enlighten her. Not entirely convinced, Harriet summoned up a grateful smile, thanked her hostess and continued with her preparations.

All the dresses were silk with a gossamer overlay giving them an iridescent quality. Harriet's was emerald — with her red hair and green eyes, the obvious choice — and she loved it. It whispered when she moved, flowing out and around her slender frame as though liquid, even her shoes matched.

The duchess had gone to great lengths to make this perfect. Heaven only knew how much it had cost, and now Roger was indisposed by which, Harriet guessed, meant he had been at one of the gaming hells or gentleman's clubs and drunk himself into a stupor.

Indisposed? Pfft, purely self-inflicted. She hoped he had a really sore head. Now, she would be compelled to dance with some stranger, and her mother would be watching, and the whole thing would be a farce.

She shook her head and swivelled to face the mirror as Phyllis, the maid allocated to assist, buttoned up the gown and began to tame Harriet's wild tresses into something resembling a presentable style.

Chapter Nine

N ot far away, Jasper was sitting in front of the fire in his study, the leaping flames reminding him of how he used to make pictures from them when a child.

The warmth of the room was soporific, the ponderous ticking of the grandfather clock, hypnotic. His lids grew heavy and despite his best efforts, felt himself drifting off.

About to slip over the edge into sleep, Jasper became aware of a cool draught on his face — odd, was not the door was closed? As he turned his head to check, he swore a hand cupped his cheek.

He must be dreaming. Confirmed seconds later.

"What are you doing Jasper?" a familiar voice demanded in his mind. *"Do not let her go because you are scared of losing her, scared she will say no to what you wish to offer, scared she might die. Stop hiding behind me, I need to leave, your fear is keeping me bound to you, and I am so very tired."*

A long pause, then, *"Jasper, we loved each other but it was a safe, comfortable love. You love Harriet with an all-consuming passion, enduring and irrevocable, and if you do not tell her, your heart will remain frozen.*

This is not living, 'tis scarcely even existing, and you will wither away. Harriet loves you, you know she does, please tell her you return her love, tell her every day from now until your last breath, and let me rest."

The voice faded.

Jasper murmured her name, "Emmeline…"

"Go to her Jasper… Jasper… ***Jasper…* Jasper!***"

Jasper bolted upright, as a hand shook his shoulder, roughly.

"Jasper, wake up, you're needed."

It was Joanna.

Jasper stared at his sister in bewilderment. What just happened? He couldn't seem to focus, and Joanna was still shaking him. "Joanna. What? What is so important you need wrench my shoulder from its socket?"

"You must go to the ball. Lord Roger, Harry's partner, is unwell. Something has upset his delicate constitution. More likely he had one too many whiskys last night," Joanna's derisive tones making her contempt for the young man quite clear. "Anyway, apparently, he is laid low and will not be able to attend. You have to come, Jasper, she needs you."

Jasper glowered at his sister. "She does not need me. There are likely any number of men willing to prostrate themselves before her, hoping she might scatter a crumb in their direction. Have one of them take Pelham's place."

"Jasper Algernon Ogilvie, get upstairs this instant and prepare for the evening. You will *not* behave like this towards Harry. You know you love her and, heaven help her, she loves you too. Emmeline is dead, she died four years ago. It was a terrible accident and there was nothing you could have done to prevent it. It was tragic, but it was a long time ago, and she would be dumbfounded if she could see you now."

"Now will you do as I ask?" A ghost of an echo, faint but no less insistent. *"Harriet is the one to rescue your heart, you just need to let her."*

Jasper jumped out of the chair and spun around, certain he

would see Emmeline in the room but, of course, there was nothing, except perhaps a slight movement of the heavy brocade framing the window. Mystified, and not entirely sure he wasn't asleep, Jasper rubbed a hand over his forehead.

Joanna was waiting, hands on hips, her expression — exasperated.

Standing in the middle of the study, Jasper ruminated on his sister's words, the words Harriet had flung at him the previous day, and the words whispered in his mind. Harriet loved him? Was that even remotely possible?

Harriet's face — her shy smile, her beautiful green eyes, and her very kissable lips — floated through his head, and he knew his sister was correct. Even if Harriet spurned him and, after yesterday, she would have every right, he had to tell her he loved her, he had to take the risk.

"Joanna Abigail Ogilvie, let us say your words are true, I fear 'tis too late. Yesterday, she left believing me to be embarrassed by her. Why should she even see me, let alone dance with me?"

"Because, she gave me this, which I was supposed to keep until the morrow, but I think you should open it now." Joanna handed him Harriet's gift. "Moreover, 'tis Christmas, and magic happens. Now go." She shooed him out of the room and up the stairs, before ringing for his valet to assist his preparations.

In the privacy of his bedchamber, Jasper unwrapped the box to find nestled within, a leather-bound book. Opening it — the cover creaking with age — he read the title, a wry grin twitching his lips. On the flyleaf Harriet had written,

I never wanted to be tamed but, curiously, I found it to be the most exhilarating experience of my life, and I never want it to end.

Yours, Harriet.

Jasper traced the words and, as his valet entered the room, all his eminently sensible arguments fell away.

The maelstrom in his mind calmed, and his heart lifted.

In a quiet room in a sumptuous house on one of the most fashionable squares in London, Harriet Winterbourne was fighting the impulse to chew her nails to the quick. Only the thought of what her mother would say prevented her. There were mere moments left before the performance, and Harriet had no partner.

Where was this alleged understudy? Grrrr, when she got her hands on Lord Roger Pelham, a sore head would be the least of his worries. Lady Hereford would have to excuse her. Perhaps this waltz was forever destined to have only nine ladies dancing.

Half of her was glad. It meant she wouldn't spoil the dance for the others by making an idiot of herself. The other half, her stubborn, perverse and wilful side, was desperate to prove to her naysayers that she could, in fact, dance.

She was about to seek out the duchess when there came a knock on the door. A maid peeped in to say the replacement had arrived, was adding the final touches to his attire, and Lady Harriet was not to fret.

Torn between relief and abject panic, Harriet nodded her thanks, and tried to steady her trembling hands. She glanced in the mirror to ensure her mask was in place and, with one last brush of her skirts, muttered, "Well, I am as ready as I'll ever be." Grimacing fiercely at her reflection, making Phyllis giggle.

"Get on with you, my lady. You look lovely, you will outshine the rest of them and no mistake."

"I shall do no such thing, but thank you for thinking I might, Phyllis." She chuckled, then drew a deep breath. "Wish me luck?"

"You don't need luck, Lady Harriet, but I gladly wish it for you."

Harriet grinned and walked purposefully along the many

corridors to the edge of the ballroom. All the ladies stood at one side, the gentlemen lined up opposite.

They waited, twittering nervously while Lady Hereford announced the entertainment.

"My lords, ladies, and gentlemen, four years ago, we lost a bright star. Lady Emmeline Fortescue was killed two days before the Christmas Ball and, out of respect, we decided not to replace her in the waltz, leaving us with nine ladies.

"Although, no longer quite so risqué a dance, this year, I felt it appropriate to reprise the performance, but with ten couples as intended originally. For a brief moment, I feared the past was about to repeat itself when one of our number was stuck down by an unknown illness this afternoon."

There were a few gasps.

"Fortuitously, we were able to persuade someone with a personal connection, to step into the breach."

Harriet frowned. *What a strange thing to say, who could it be?* Something tugged at the back of her mind, but she was so nervous, she could not ponder its significance long enough to pin it down. She forced herself to listen as the duchess introduced them.

"Without further ado, I give you — the waltz."

Ten ladies stepped forward and, across the dance floor, ten men did the same. As the strains of Mozart's hauntingly beautiful music filled the ballroom, they moved to their positions.

From his place opposite Harriet, Jasper was entranced. Her dress was the perfect complement to her burnished locks, which were barely restrained in an exotic style and somewhat concealed behind her mask. He could see the tremor in her hands even from the other side of the room, and itched to hold them, to calm her.

Steadily, he walked towards her.

Harriet waited, lashes lowered, but when he reached her, she lifted her head to greet her new partner. Their eyes collided — vivid green on molten chocolate, and he saw Harriet's widen in surprise.

"J-Jasper?" She stammered. "What... wait... how...?" Her questions died, as the orchestra paused in readiness.

Jasper placed his right hand on her waist and clasped the fingers of her right hand into his left.

Baffled, Harriet rested her left hand on his right shoulder and they began to dance.

Chapter Ten

A t first, Harriet counted the beat, terrified she would lose her step and have to listen to her mother berate her well into the new year but, with Jasper, she didn't need to.

It was as though they were born to waltz together and, notwithstanding their argument — to be fair, her tantrum — of the previous day, they moved as one around the floor.

"Please accept my apologies for my appalling behaviour yesterday," Jasper murmured in her ear as they executed a perfect turn.

She raised her eyes to look at him but said nothing. What was she supposed to say? Dropping her gaze, she stared fixedly at the top of his arm, which did not help given she could see his muscles flexing under the fine material of his jacket while they danced.

Harriet's confusion aside, all her hard work was worth it, for they swirled around the room, weaving among the other couples with effortless grace, letting the music guide their steps.

The shimmering silk of the gowns appeared almost luminous in the candlelight. Their iridescence reflected in the jewel-like adornments on the masks, which, in turn, scattered rainbows of colour around an audience transfixed.

"I admit I panicked."

Her eyes shot back to his and she very nearly stumbled. Only Jasper's quick reaction prevented an embarrassing gaffe.

"You *panicked*?" she hissed, feeling her temper begin to flare again. She sucked in a steadying breath. "Oh, my lord, please do not insult my intelligence."

Realising this might take rather longer than one waltz, Jasper wracked his brain for the words to make her believe it was because he feared the judgemental eyes of Society, not that he didn't want to be seen with her.

"Harriet, my tactless rejection of your invitation was owing to my own insecurities. It has been so long since I mixed with my peers, it became easier to remain a recluse than deal with a constant barrage of questions from meddlesome gossips, and well-meant platitudes from friends who had no idea what to say. You were the only one who refused to let me wallow and I did not wish to subject you to what I assumed would be akin to an inquisition."

Another turn. His hand fell back on her waist. "I cannot imagine anything more wonderful than dancing with you..." he hesitated. Emmeline's words filtered through his mind, and Jasper opened his heart, "...forever."

Harriet did stumble then. Thankfully, Jasper caught her before she lost her step completely, certain she heard her mother grinding her teeth.

"I fear I misheard you, my lord. Pray would you be kind enough to repeat that?" she husked, holding his gaze as they floated through their last turn. The hammering of her heart seemed indecently loud. *How was not the whole of Society deafened?*

In the centre of the ballroom, as the last notes died away, Jasper blatantly ignored the prepared finale, and dipped Harriet.

He smiled wickedly at her startled squeak, her sylphlike figure describing a perfect arc.

He held her there for several seconds, to delighted sighs from all the ladies in the audience, before slowly bringing her upright.

As their eyes met, he said, "I love you."

His declaration fell into that curious moment of silence between the end of a performance and the applause.

Everyone heard.

Murmurs of astonishment ensued, along with one very nervous giggle, none of which Jasper or Harriet were aware. As they continued to stare at each other, the same hush descended.

"Y-you l-love me?" Harriet stuttered, incredulously.

"With all my heart," came his candid reply.

With nerveless fingers, Harriet removed Jasper's mask, captivated by the profound emotion in his eyes. Exquisite tendrils of heat coiled through her.

Jasper mirrored her actions and the instant her mask was off, he kissed her.

Uncaring that they were in the middle of Lady Hereford's ballroom, that every member of the *ton* was witnessing his audacious behaviour, and that Harriet's mother announced she was about to swoon from the scandal, Jasper continued to kiss Harriet until she was convinced they were spinning somewhere amongst the stars.

Thunderous applause and more than a few cheers obliterated shocked gasps.

Jasper broke their kiss and stroked one finger along Harriet's suddenly rosy cheeks. He held her close and dropped another kiss on her forehead.

The applause died down.

Harriet stepped out of his arms to dip a flawless curtsy. It could not have been easy for Jasper to bare his heart in front of all these people; she owed him the same courtesy.

Taking his hand, she smiled up at him and, leaving no one in any doubt, said quietly but firmly,

"I love you too."

Riveted on the couple, the audience erupted again, and it was several moments before Lady Hereford was able to make herself heard over the uproar. Eventually, everyone settled down and gave their attention to their hostess.

"I would like to thank my couples for their hard work in preparing for tonight's performance, which has concluded in quite the most unforeseen manner and, for my part, I am certain Lady Emmeline would approve wholeheartedly."

She added her appreciation to all those involved, but Jasper and Harriet were no longer listening.

"I do believe she is correct. I think Emmeline would be pleased. If it did not make me sound deranged, I swear she spoke to me the afternoon I fell in the Serpentine. I had to check three times to make sure she was not standing in the bedchamber next to me." Harriet's cheeks glowed, hearing the nonsensical words trip off her tongue

"'Tis curious, but I too have sensed her presence recently, since we started practising if I'm honest. I presumed it was the time of year. Normally, I would never admit to believing in ghosts but..." he left that dangling, unable to articulate exactly what he had experienced.

"She told me I was the one to rescue your heart," Harriet confessed, shyly.

"She told me, if I did not tell you how much I love you, my heart would remain frozen." Jasper's expression, confounded. "Was it her? Is what I am, what we are, saying even plausible?"

He shook his head. "Listen to us, daring to entertain the idea that someone who has been dead four years spoke not only to me but also to you. I hope to goodness no one overheard." He ran his fingers through his hair.

Harriet studied him, still reeling from his admission.

"*Was* she right? Have I?" she ventured, her wavering self-confidence requiring further affirmation.

Jasper took her hand, entwining their fingers together and drew her against him... heedless of the rules his gesture flouted. "Harriet Winterbourne, I love you with a love deeper than the restless oceans, taller than the highest mountains, and wider than the infinite heavens. My love for you is immeasurable, incalculable and fathomless. I know I am doing this the wrong way around but, if your father grants his approval, would you do me the greatest honour and consent to become my wife?"

"J-Jasper," she gulped, gawking at him in stupefaction.

"I know 'tis sudden, but it's Christmas and mayhap your magic is rubbing off on me." He twinkled, and she blushed, recalling her outburst.

"I have lost myself for too long, and refuse to waste any more of my life waiting," he hesitated, worried his proposal was overwhelming her.

Harriet was made of sterner stuff.

"Jasper Ogilvie, in truth my love for you has been smouldering for many years, but I quashed it. First, because you were bound to Emmeline, then later I presumed you saw me as a flighty debutante with nothing between her ears—"

She was interrupted by a searing kiss. "Oh my..." vainly trying to control chaotic thoughts.

"Then, when you held me while we danced, when you told me about Emmeline, when you clasped my hand, I began to hope. The day in Hyde Park before I so rudely spoilt our walk, you told me never to let go of my dream and then I knew. I knew you were the one with whom I wanted to dance for the rest of my life."

Jasper stared at her, she hadn't answered him.

Forgetting they were in the middle of the ballroom, Harriet slid cool fingers over his jawline, feeling his erratic pulse leap under her touch. Smiling her dazzling smile, she brushed her lips to his.

"Yes! One hundred, one thousand times, **yes**!"

Unaware the entire *ton* was hanging on to their every word with bated breath, Jasper and Harriet were stunned when her acceptance was met with cheers of joy.

In the corner of the room, discernible only if you looked very closely, a vaporous form began to fade.

Later in the evening, after several more dances and once he had contrived to have a quiet word with Harriet's father in the privacy of the Hereford's study, Jasper led his newly betrothed onto the terrace.

Draping a warm wrap around Harriet's shoulders, he enfolded her in his arms.

The view over the gardens was breathtaking. A stark, white scene broken here and there by apparently lifeless bushes and trees, and all sound was muffled.

It began to snow. Delicate flakes falling to earth from a laden sky, in mesmerising flurries.

"She's here," Harriet said quietly. Jasper did not need to ask whom and, even though she knew that to anyone else what she was about to say would sound ludicrous, Harriet murmured. "Thank you, Emmeline. I hope I am a worthy choice, and I promise to love Jasper from now until the end of time."

She kissed Jasper's cheek and smiled up at him, all the love she felt shining in her eyes, which sparkled in the glow cast by innumerable candles.

Feeling a little ridiculous, but nevertheless determined, Jasper added, "Emmeline, you were my first love and you will always hold a special place in my heart, but now 'tis time to move forward. I never expected to fall in love again, but I have, and I love Harriet beyond reason or explanation. Thank you for sending her to rescue my heart."

A movement in the shadows drew their attention and they noticed a faint glimmer, indistinct yet recognisable. Without thinking, Harriet curtseyed, and Jasper bowed.

"Farewell Emmeline, it is safe to let go and rest easy. I will protect his heart," Harriet whispered.

Emmeline drifted towards them, wraithlike fingers reaching out to touch their hands. She smiled, a sweet, loving smile, and as they watched, gradually vanished, leaving only a memory.

Jasper took Harriet in his arms, kissing her with intoxicating tenderness.

The clock struck midnight, welcoming in Christmas Day, as a gentle sigh came back to them on the chill night air…

"Enjoy the dance."

Catch
a
Snowflake

Author's Note

Lucas Withers has appeared in almost every one of my Regency romances. It seems only fair to tell his story... the one about how he met Jemima.

Chapter One

The ward bustled. Three orderlies were engrossed in the daily ritual of unbinding, cleaning, and redressing wounds; a harried looking doctor was trying to do six things at once, and one of the domestic staff was attempting to mop the floor, a thankless task, for it was quickly becoming strewn with bits of bandage and used cloths.

It was just after 9am on a Monday morning in early November, and Lucas Withers pushed open the door, to pause. The organised chaos confronting him was familiar, there never seemed to be an opportune time to visit his men, but he had no mind to get under the feet of those administering care.

The doctor, spotting a friendly face, waved a greeting

"Major. Good morning, sir, I'm sure the lads will be glad to see someone who is not about to add to their discomfort. Come in, man, come in. No need to loiter at the door."

"Good morning, Dr Latham. How goes it?" Lucas ventured a few more steps into the room, nodding a hello to those whom he knew in the beds closest to him. "Hendry, Peveril, following doctor's orders?" He grinned at the young men who grinned back, admitting that was indeed the case. "About time! Bit much when it takes a bullet to make you listen."

A chuckle went up at this. With slight variation, Lucas said much the same every day. He had come to realise that when he spoke to his men in a practical manner and behaved as though he expected them to be back on duty by the end of the week, they believed they would survive.

When addressed in hushed tones, with funereal sympathy, it sounded as though he was already grieving, and the men lost faith in their chances.

Taking the seat by the desk at the end of the ward, he waited until Dr Latham had finished his rounds, whereupon the two had a brief discussion about the prognosis of the soldiers Lucas had come to check on. Along with Hendry and Peveril, there were two others.

One was a captain, close to his own age who had received terrible burns in an ambush and was currently in a side room. A young and — burns aside — healthy individual, he was responding to treatment and, although bore close monitoring, the powers that be hoped he might be able to go home for a short visit at Christmas.

The other, a young private named Jack Parsons. Jack, assigned to Lucas' regiment a matter of months previously, was injured when a piece of flying shrapnel — the result of a ricochet from a French bullet — lodged in his leg.

Not fatal, in and of itself, but the appalling conditions in the field hospitals meant death by disease was more likely than death by wound. Parsons had succumbed to a virulent infection and, for a while, it was touch and go.

He rallied enough to be transported back to England since when he had been under Latham's care at St Bart's — a hospital which had become well versed in treating the horrific wounds typical of war during the past decade or so. In the clean and more sterile conditions of the ward, Parsons had responded well, and the doctor was confident the young soldier would recover.

Lucas knew the boy had a sister who visited him, but their paths had yet to cross. He walked over to chat with Parsons, musing as to why he kept missing her.

This paragon, whose praises Jack sang at every opportunity was the only family member of his soldiers, still incapacitated and confined to St Bart's, whom he had not met. He would like to make her acquaintance.

Lucas believed it was important to speak with the relatives of his men. Many did not understand what their sons, fathers, husbands, or brothers had witnessed, endured, and suffered, and a quiet word sometimes went a long way to helping all parties readjust to a life far removed from the battlefield.

Pushing it aside for now, he sat by the narrow hospital bed, major and private soon engaged in lively debate. They covered a variety of topics from the social unrest beginning to plague the country, to whether Lord Byron's accusations against Lord Castlereagh were valid, particularly given the latter's stringent and tireless efforts at diplomacy.

Neither heard the approach of light footsteps, until Lucas detected a breath of fragrance. Something delicate, bringing to mind spring blossoms. *Spring blossoms, really?*

He shook his head to dispatch the notion and turned in his chair, springing to his feet when he noticed a composed young woman moving to stand at the other side of Jack's bed. She was smiling down at the soldier with such loving tenderness, Lucas felt his chest tighten.

"Morning, Jack. No, don't get up, just you lie there and let people rush about pandering to your every whim." The woman patted Jack's arm, as she sank onto the edge of the bed.

"Major Withers, sir. May I introduce my sister, Miss Jemima Parsons? Jemima, my commanding officer, Major Lucas Withers." Jack waved his hand between the two.

Jemima's cool appraisal made the tall and, had he realised it, ruggedly handsome soldier waiting to greet her, frown. Lucas could not think what he had done in the last two minutes to prompt such a reserved reaction.

"'Tis a pleasure to meet you, Miss Parsons." He bowed but kept his distance. He had the oddest impression, she was boiling mad and had no mind to put himself in the firing line, he had seen too much of that.

"I wish I could say the feeling is mutual, but I would be lying. I am sure you have other hapless victims to torment. Might you be so kind as to do so?"

Lucas felt his jaw drop. *What the devil?* Her dismissive words and narrowed eyes made her low regard abundantly clear, but he was at a loss as to the reason.

"I beg your pardon, Miss Parsons. My intent was not to cause upset." He fixed his gaze on his subordinate. "Take care, Jack. I shall pop in before I leave."

"Please do not waste your time, *Major* Withers," she sneered his military rank. "Jack does not need your sympathy. You have done enough."

"*Jemima*," Jack hissed. "You forget yourself. Sir, please forgive my sister she is… well it's just that…" he trailed off. There was no excusing Jemima's rudeness.

"Fret not, Private. 'Tis a rare day, I allow a moment's impudence to trouble me. Rest easy, I will look you up when next I am passing. Although, I shall ensure you are alone."

He winked at the red-faced young man and went to ask whether he might be able to have a few minutes with William Harcourt, the burn victim. Walking down the ward, he heard Jack berating his sister, and Jemima refusing to apologise.

When he reached the door, Lucas turned and, for no reason he could think of, stood for a moment, observing the siblings. Heads together while they argued, their likeness was undeniable, although Miss Parsons was a darker, more vibrant version of her brother.

As though she sensed his scrutiny, Jemima lifted her head and their eyes locked. Lucas watched her hand flutter to her throat, his gaze drawn to her slender neck and porcelain skin, at the same time as he became aware his heart was beating far more erratically than was warranted.

Unsure what was happening, Lucas Withers inclined his head ever so slightly, spun on his heel, and left the ward.

Chapter Two

"Jemima. What was all that about?" Jack demanded when Major Withers strode away.

"If not for him, you would not be stuck in a hospital bed," Jemima retorted, taking care to keep her voice low. She glanced around the ward. All these men their lives forever blighted because of the stupidity of a few.

"How many times do I have to tell you, it was not Major Withers' fault I was hit," Jack countered. "He did not fire the gun. He and Lieutenant Bertran carried me over a mile to the medic. Honestly, girl, sometimes you should hold that recalcitrant tongue of yours."

"Jack?" Jemima was taken aback by the vehemence in her brother's tone.

Jack strove to curb his temper. He loved Jemima, but once she got a bee in her bonnet it was very hard to persuade her to see sense.

"Jem, Major Withers is a good man. One of the best. Everyone wanted to serve under him. He's sensible, astute, shrewd, and cares about his men. Bloody hell, he even cares about the horses. Me and me mates swore he got all teary one evening because we had to shoot his favourite stallion. Poor critter was terrible lame, the mud you know."

As though Jemima was cognisant with the acres of stinking quagmires scattered with rotting flesh and other unmentionables that were the battlefields of France.

Jemima squirmed, uncomfortably. She had been, in her opinion, righteously furious for what felt like an age, blaming the military hierarchy for dragging out the war long enough that her little brother went and joined up, and it was difficult to rein it in.

After a protracted silence, she huffed an aggrieved sigh, and muttered, not very graciously, "Fine. I shall apologise. But do not expect me to like him," she warned.

Jack smothered a grin at her mutinous expression. "Go, be penitent. He's probably gone to visit Cap'n Harcourt. Be mindful though, the cap'n is a mess. Badly burned by a unit of damn *crapauds*," he spat the last word, using the British military slang for the French soldiers — toads.

"Beg pardon, Jem. It's just the cap'n, he's like the major, quite bookish really, more thinker than killer and what they did to him... I don't know whether he'll ever recover." He shuddered, his words demonstrating an unexpected maturity.

Jemima gripped his hand. "Do not think on it, Jack. Here comes Isaac with coffee. Enjoy that, and I shall be back in the blink of an eye." Jemima grinned at Isaac, one of the orderlies, and, reluctantly, went in search of Lucas Withers.

After peering into several rooms, all of which were empty, Jemima surmised the Major must have left. Then, she came to a short corridor leading off the main hallway. This annexe was quiet, almost unnervingly so, a sentiment not alleviated when Jemima thought she discerned an occasional moan.

She hesitated, uncertain now. It wasn't fair to barge in on some poor injured soldier just because Jack felt she ought to apologise to his commanding officer. About to retrace her steps, Jemima heard the soft click of a door, and saw the subject of her thoughts moving with haste towards her.

"Miss Parsons?" Major Withers' hushed tones were laced with mild astonishment. Unwilling to raise her voice, Jemima waited until he reached her.

"I came to apologise for my churlish behaviour." She held his gaze, then her head dropped. "It's just…" she stared down at her hands which she was twisting together, trying to find the words to explain her irrational fear without sounding like a petulant child.

"'Tis frightening, is it not?"

At his gentle question, her head shot up and she stared into his face. It was a kindly face she realised, if rather craggy and wearied. His dark blue eyes held hers, and she saw no censure despite her appalling manners.

She nodded, slowly. "Jack is all I have left. Our parents died within a year of each other and, since then, it has just been him and me against the world. Then he got the stupid idea to join up, of going off to fight. What did he think was going to happen? No one comes back unscathed. Even those fortunate not to be injured are still wounded."

Jemima sucked in a steadying breath, unsure why she was telling a complete stranger this. "That said, he assures me you are a good man who did not deserve my wrath, for which I am sincerely sorry."

"War is destructive in so many ways, Miss Parsons. I found no joy in sending men to what could easily be their deaths, and you are correct, none of us is unscathed. I am surprised we have not met before now. Had we done so, I might have been able to mitigate some of your distress, by answering what I surmise would be many questions concerning Jack. I am here most every day, usually later I must admit, but I have an unavoidable commitment this afternoon."

"I tend to come after morning rounds. I spend some time with Jack, then see whether any of the others would like me to read or help them write a letter or just talk." She shrugged. "'Tis only a couple of hours every other day, not much to give, but seems to cheer them."

"I imagine a visit from someone as beautiful as you, would be enough to cheer even the most melancholy of souls."

Jemima flicked him a sharp glance, but his features were smooth. No sign he was jesting. Perplexed, her brow creased. From anyone else the words would sound over-familiar, or trite but, from Lucas Withers, they did not appear calculated, more it was simply his opinion — candid and unfeigned, as though he meant it. Jemima felt heat wash up her cheeks. No one had called her beautiful before, and she never considered herself anything other than ordinary.

"Errr… thank you, errr… Major, sir," she stammered, feeling inordinately shy.

"Please call me Lucas. I suspect we shall run into each other from time to time as we have a mutual concern for Jack. All this formality will get in the way of what we actually want to talk about." He smiled then, and it lit his whole face.

"In that case, please call me Jemima." She could not refuse him this.

"Thank you, 'tis a lovely name. I…"

Just then, a low groan reached them, interrupting Lucas' train of thought.

"Please excuse me, I should get back to Harcourt, I have already tarried rather longer than I intended."

Chapter Three

"Is he the soldier who was badly burned?" She saw Lucas' quizzical expression. "Jack told me it was likely him on whom you were checking. Were you on your way to fetch something?" Jemima queried, recalling his purposeful stride.

"Yes, I was going to fill this pot. 'Tis a balm to smooth over his skin." He showed Jemima the small pot he was holding in his left hand. Almost empty save a thin coating around the sides, but enough for a subtle blend of aromas to tickle her nostrils.

"Do I detect flaxseed, honey and… is that myrrh?" Jemima essayed.

Impressed, Lucas raised an eyebrow. "Yes. You have a good nose. Not many pick up on myrrh."

"I find the fragrance soothing. I have a small bottle, just one drop on a handkerchief is enough to settle a fractious stomach, or dispatch a threatening headache. Oh, 'tis good for all manner of maladies. This is the first I have heard it being used for burns." Her tone invited clarification, which Lucas — who for reasons he could not fathom was relishing this brief interlude — provided.

"It helps reduce the chance of infection and aids faster healing. Moreover, maybe you are correct in that the scent also calms fretful nerves. Poor Harcourt has a long road ahead of him, and I imagine his patience will be stretched to its limits, if indeed he recovers."

"There remains some doubt?" Jemima asked.

"You can never tell with burns. They appear to be healing, but infection often lurks under the damaged skin, unseen until it is too late." He waved the pot again. "Hence the myrrh. Mind, he's a stubborn devil, he'll survive just to prove the naysayers wrong."

Lucas grinned, and Jemima was beset by an impulse to help in any way she could.

"Permit me to sit with him, while you do whatever it is you need to do. I might not be able to heal his wounds, but mayhap I can distract him from the pain until you return."

"Are you sure? 'Tis not a sight I would wish on a gentlewoman."

"I am not easily upset, Maj… Lucas. I should be glad to."

Not convinced this self-possessed young lady comprehended exactly what she was letting herself in for, Lucas acquiesced and led her along to the door, through which she had seen him exit.

Opening it, he ushered her inside, his quietly repeated, "are you sure?" receiving a nod.

The room was cool and dim, the shutters were closed, a single candle the only light. On the bed lay a man whose features would give most people nightmares. Half of his face was handsome, unmarred, the other, a grotesque mask of melted flesh. The burn ran from his forehead, down his face, across his neck to his shoulder.

Where it had blistered, the tortured flesh was puckered, and Jemima spied one or two areas where the skin was weeping. How his right eye and his nose had avoided damage was nothing short of a miracle, although she reckoned the soldier would not consider anything about his injuries, miraculous.

"We allow the skin to breathe between applications of this

ointment. After about half an hour, we reapply and re-bandage," Lucas murmured close to her ear.

"Will he mind me talking to him?" Jemima replied in the same low tone, ignoring the curious frisson which ran down her spine when his breath brushed her neck.

"I daresay he will prefer to listen to you than me." Lucas chuckled softly. "I shall return forthwith."

"Do not hurry on my account. I have nowhere else to be." She turned her attention to the man lying so still on the narrow bed.

"Hello, sir. My name is Jemima. I am very happy to meet you, and wondered whether you had any objection to my keeping you company while Major Withers attends to an important task?"

Captain Harcourt did not reply, but a reflexive movement in his left hand, told Jemima he had heard.

She glanced up at Lucas. "I will be fine, go."

She smiled, and Lucas felt a corresponding warmth in his chest, at the same time as the world felt as though it was shifting under his feet.

Shaking his head, to rid it of confusion, Lucas hurried from the room.

Unaware of the effect, her smile had on Lucas, Jemima was concentrating on Captain Harcourt. Modulating her voice, she began to talk about anything and nothing, starting by portraying the scene outside. How, overnight there had been sharp frost, the silvery rime coating everything, turning a dull city into something quite spectacular.

She chattered in this vein for several minutes, then moved on to describe the revelry of the winter fair, concluding with, "They are predicting snow before the week's out. I love the snow. Even though it can be a hinderance to many people, you know, tradesmen and the like, a little delay here and there is worth it for the chance to witness such beauty. Have you ever looked at a snowflake?"

She didn't expect an answer and was gratified when she caught a flicker of his eyelids. "They are like minuscule pieces of the most fragile lace, made from cobwebs. Each one is different. Did you know that? To be lucky enough to catch one and see its exquisite delicacy before it melts, is like a gift from God." She blushed a little.

Engrossed, Jemima had no idea Lucas had returned and was standing in the doorway listening to her. Her words conjured up a scene so clearly, it could have been right in front of him, instead of a darkened room where a man clung to life.

He was seized by a sudden desire to linger in a park when the snow began to fall, in the hope he might chance to study a snowflake.

Deliberately scraping his boot on the wooden floor, so she would be aware of his presence, Lucas crossed the room and sat at the opposite side of the bed from Jemima. Taking the lid off the pot, he began to massage the balm gently over the captain's skin. First, his face, then his arms.

Jemima managed to repress her horrified gasp when she saw the furrowed welts on the underside of the captain's right arm.

"He tried to shield his face," Lucas explained.

Silently, Jemima dipped her hands in a bowl of water standing on the little table at the head of the bed and wiped them dry on a convenient cloth. Without asking for permission, she stretched over and scooped out a sizeable dollop of the balm.

Lifting the captain's left arm, she studied it speculatively, trying to see whether there was a better direction along which to apply the ointment. Determining from elbow to wrist looked like the path of least resistance — and with no outward sign that her stomach was roiling — Jemima copied Lucas' gestures.

She talked while she worked, hoping to distract the patient from what must have been an excruciatingly painful ordeal.

She was rinsing residual ointment from her fingers, when the captain opened his eyes.

"Good morning, sir. Forgive us for waking you. The major here is just re-bandaging your wounds and then you can enjoy an undisturbed rest for a little while."

"You said there will be snow," his speech sounded a little slurred. Partly because he was barely conscious and partly because the right corner of his mouth had not escaped the flames.

"The weatherwise say by week's end. Although the air was a little sour today, mayhap it will be earlier," Jemima affirmed, nothing in her demeanour to indicate how pleased she was that not only had he heard her patter, but also felt moved to respond. "If you like, when it does, I'll bring you a snowflake."

There was a rumble of laughter. "I think it will melt long before you can carry it here," Captain Harcourt said, "but I thank you for being so kind as to suggest it."

He added, almost absently, "It would be nice to feel the cool of snow on my face." He sighed, offered a hint of a smile, and closed his eyes.

Lucas watched for a few moments, noting the steady rise and fall of the captain's chest.

"Thank you, Jemima."

"What did I do?"

"Gave him hope."

Chapter Four

Over the following days, a pattern unfolded. Once she had spent her usual time with Jack, and the other soldiers she visited, Jemima sat with Captain Harcourt.

Upon leaving St Bart's, the morning she first became acquainted with Lucas Withers, Jemima swung by her favourite book shop — The Wise Owl, just off Shaftesbury Avenue — and purchased a selection she hoped might pique the captain's interest.

Along with Chaucer and Shakespeare, she found an English translation of Madam d'Aulnoy's *Les Contes de Fées*, and a volume of similar tales by Charles Perrault, both of which she loved, reasoning that while they may not be tales for soldiers, they were cleverly written, and all included a bit of adventure.

Jemima was also excited to be in possession of a very recent publication, *Waverly*, by an anonymous author — a tale set around the Jacobite rebellion of 1745. She presumed this would be more appealing to the men than perhaps were the fairy tales — grateful to her friend, Lucy, who worked at the book shop, and who kept aside any new publications.

A varied collection of books amassed, Jemima enjoyed being able to offer her listeners a choice of story.

Those who were able, were often found around the fire at the end of the ward, wrapped snugly in blankets to stave off any chill, entertained by the myriad of worlds, Jemima wove around them.

The few who struggled to leave their beds did not miss out, for she was as happy reading to one as several and, if Jemima was known to be in the hospital and not on either of the two main wards, they need only to check Captain Harcourt's room, the latter showing a marked improvement since Jemima had included him in, what the patients humorously called, her book club.

It did snow, heavily, making the journey to and from St Bart's, arduous. Jemima refused to allow such a thing as the weather prevent her from visiting her charges, and trudged through the thickening snow every day.

It was tiring, but a little fatigue was nothing compared with what those on the wards had suffered, and Jemima knew, without being conceited, that her presence added interest to their day. More so because she was not prodding and poking at their wounds than for any other reason.

She had not seen Lucas Withers since the day she was introduced to Captain Harcourt but, to her chagrin, his face insisted on popping into her head at the most inopportune moments. Like when she was reading from Perrault's *Cendrillon* and she came to the description of the prince.

While the hero of the tale sounded in no way similar to Lucas in looks, it was the essence of the character which resembled the major. A man handsome in deeds as well as face.

His image superimposed itself on the page, blurring the words and, frustrated with herself for such feminine nonsense, Jemima clapped the book shut and sought a broadsheet. Political and social news would surely be enough to divert her flighty head.

Unbeknownst to Jemima, Lucas was wrestling with much the same problem. Jemima's beautiful hazel eyes, darkening to grey as she glared at him over Jack's head, warming to tawny when she assured him, she would be fine watching over Harcourt, were etched into his mind.

He had met her but once, yet she lingered in his thoughts, taunting him when least expected. In light of this, Lucas made the deliberate decision not to attend St Barts in the mornings, hoping that by avoiding the possibility of coming face-to-face with Jemima, he would forget her.

It was a vain hope.

A month before Christmas, and everywhere was covered in a blanket of white. All sound was muffled, even the rattling of carriages became muted. It was just after midday, and Lucas was strolling along Hosier Lane to St Bart's.

As he turned onto West Smithfield, a most bizarre sight confronted him, and in the frigid air of the December afternoon, he questioned whether his brain had frozen.

A tree was walking towards him.

He halted in his tracks, and studied the oddity, realising, with more than a modicum of relief, the 'tree' was wearing sturdy boots. Waiting until the profusion of boughs reached him, he was unable to prevent a bark of laughter when he realised the footwear belonged to Jemima Parsons.

"Why, Miss Parsons. I am very glad to see 'tis you, not a tree grown legs," he greeted her.

Jemima peered at him through arms full of deep green fronds, and grinned, a little self-consciously.

"I know 'tis early, but a few decorations will brighten the wards, and the scent of pine is very uplifting." She shuffled to get a better grip of her burden. "I have brought some paper — gold and silver — which I hope the men might be persuaded to cut into shapes like stars or bells, as well as some red material for bows.

"It might seem trivial and a bit childish, but it gives the patients something different to do, and will offer a lovely contrast with the green. Dr Latham assured me they would not feel foolish," she added this, doubtfully, suddenly concerned Lucas might think her plan a bit insulting to men who had served in wars.

"I think 'tis a marvellous idea. Please allow me to carry some of that for you." Lucas took most of the fronds from Jemima, who blew a sigh.

"Thank you. They were becoming heavy." She smiled and tucked a long strand of hair behind her left ear, the gesture drawing Lucas' gaze.

By sheer force of will, he banished the almost irresistible temptation to kiss the tender spot, and hurried her through the wintery streets. Moments later they were in the comparative warmth of St Bart's.

The ward was quiet, all the usual duties completed prior to lunch, and the men were scattered about the ward. Some were by the fire, some around the huge table, some sitting by the bedside of friends, others slept. Those who were awake, looked up when Jemima and Lucas entered, and all wore matching expressions of astonishment.

It was so comical, neither Lucas nor Jemima dared glance at the other. Stifling her mirth, Jemima pointed to a corner of the room where Dr Latham said she could lay the boughs, while she decorated the two wards.

Despite a distinct lack of enthusiasm from the convalescents,

Jemima was not to be thwarted. Thus, with considerable grumbling and complaint that such tasks were for womenfolk — which earned them a tut and a frown — the men found themselves embroiled in all manner of creativity.

While they were busy, Jemima vanished, to return shortly thereafter carrying some sprigs of holly laden with red berries.

While the men cut and folded, snipped and twisted — paper and material — Jemima and Lucas, whom she had coaxed into helping, placed boughs of bay, ivy, and holly, interspersed with an occasional branch of pine, on every available window ledge, on the top of cupboards and bookcases, and along the mantel.

Then she went across the corridor and did the same in that ward. These two rooms, specifically dedicated to returned servicemen — both army and navy, frequently housed long-term patients due to the nature of their injuries, and many missed out on seasonal festivities. Jemima was determined that this Christmas, they wouldn't.

Chapter Five

S atisfied, she had done all she could in the two wards, Jemima made her way along the cool, dim hall to the room where Captain Harcourt lay. Knocking quietly, she opened the door and, to her delight, saw the captain was sitting up.

"Good afternoon, sir. Would you like me to add some festive cheer to your accommodation? While I cannot hope to emulate Mivart's or the Clarendon, I think you might be suitably impressed by my artistic efforts."

She grinned engagingly at the ailing soldier who, unexpectedly, felt himself grin back.

"There you go. A smile, even a small one, is the best start to an afternoon." She chattered on guilelessly, throwing out an odd question with respect to placement of greenery, making sure the room had enough that it looked seasonal without becoming overwhelming.

Jemima had fabricated several balls of mistletoe, white berries a lovely contrast with the red and green ribbon entwined around its long branch. In a moment of heady recklessness — brought on, she claimed, by the pervading sense of goodwill — she stretched over the bed.

Holding a spare sprig of mistletoe over the captain's head, she brushed her lips to his unscarred cheek.

"I wish you the most blessed of Yuletides, and hope you are restored to full health before the new year is half out."

"Thank you, Jemima. If I could be healed by the sight of your cheerful countenance, I would be bounding along the Serpentine as we speak." He smiled, the curious quirk of his damaged lip giving him an impish quality.

Unbidden, Jemima found herself whispering a silent, extra wish that soon, he might find someone to love him without reserve or condition.

She did not hear Lucas open the door, and therefore missed the expression which flitted across his face at the sight of her kissing his subordinate.

Taking in, what looked like a moment of intimacy, Lucas felt his chest pinch, and an unfamiliar emotion soured his mouth — jealousy. *Good god was he jealous of William? The poor blighter needed someone like Jemima to coax him back to life.*

Lucas knew she visited him whenever she came to the hospital, because William never failed to mention how she enlivened his day. That she might be developing an affection for the soldier, had never entered Lucas' head until this moment.

Her gesture served to solidify what he had been trying so hard to ignore. *He had gone and fallen in love with Jemima. How was that even possible?* They had spent scarcely any time together, their conversations, of necessity, circling wounds and treatments — neither being conducive to the notion of proposing a courtship.

None of that mattered.

Lucas Withers, twenty-eight years old, veteran of many campaigns, a man who judged himself too set in his ways and too jaded for anything as frivolous as romance, had just lost the battle for his heart. *Hell, and damnation.*

Pulling himself together — he would never jeopardise the chance for William to find that one person who would love him regardless of his injuries — Lucas coughed lightly to alert the two, now deep in conversation, to his presence.

"Oh, Lucas, how fortuitous. Just when I need someone tall, here you are. Please would you hook this," Jemima waved the mistletoe ball, "over that?" Pointing to the curtain rail, above and to the right of William's head. Lucas did as she asked before taking his usual seat by the bed.

"How are you feeling today, Harcourt?" he asked the captain, forcing his attention back to the practical.

"Fair to middling," William replied. "Jemima is intent on turning my room into an arboretum but otherwise, no news to speak of." A wry smile accompanied his words. "I am hoping to be granted permission to spend a few days at home soon. It will be nice to see something other than these four walls."

"Captain Harcourt, how wonderful. Do you have family…?" Jemima trailed off. She had never seen anyone other than Lucas, the hospital staff or herself visit William. "My apologies, I…"

"Do not fret, Jemima. No, my parents are dead, there is only me. My home is quiet save my staff, but to be in my own bed is something I desire greatly."

"I can only imagine." Jemima patted his arm and bustled about adding the finishing touches to her decorations; tucking red bows here and there among the pine and bay.

She stood back to survey her efforts. "Something is missing." She tapped her mouth pensively.

Her action drew Lucas' eyes to her lips, prompting another wave of temptation to wash over him. He was hard pushed not to whisk her into his arms to kiss her right there in front of Harcourt. *Control your urges, man*, he instructed himself, sternly, *she is not for you.*

"Got it, be right back." She flew from the room, leaving the faint echo of her footsteps and the light fragrance that Lucas had come to recognise was quintessentially Jemima, in her wake.

"She will make someone a good wife," William remarked absently. "Mind, I hope whoever wins her does not quash that vitality."

Lucas stared at him in puzzlement. "Are you not…?" He wasn't quite sure how to phrase what he assumed. Men rarely discussed matters of the heart.

William barked with laughter. "I? Good lord, no." Noting a frown beginning to form on his commander's brow, he hastened to clarify.

"Make no mistake, sir, she is quite lovely, but my affection for Jemima is nothing more than that of a friend, possibly bordering on the fraternal. She has made my days here less arduous, and there is no doubt she possesses all the qualities I would wish for in a wife. Intelligent, vivacious, witty, headstrong, not to mention someone who doesn't suffer fools gladly.

"While, I imagine life with Jemima would never be dull, there is no spark between us. I had to watch my parents endure a marriage without a morsel of devotion. Yes, it was arranged as they tend to be, but I do not think they even liked each other. That I even exist continues to astonish me."

It was a long speech for a man who, since his return to England, rarely spoke more than a few words each day. He collected his thoughts.

"I will only marry if I meet a woman whose very presence lights a fire in my heart. Someone from whom I cannot bear to be apart, someone who challenges, confounds, intrigues, and bewitches. Someone, without whom my life would be less bright. I have yet to find anyone who comes close, and now," he flicked a hand towards his face, "'tis unlikely it will ever happen. It will take an extraordinary woman to see past this. I doubt such a nonpareil exists."

William's pragmatic tone made it clear he was not looking for pity, he was merely stating the facts, and Lucas had to concede he was correct. Wealth would not be enough to counteract the scarring to William's body, never mind his soul.

Chapter Six

The two men fell silent, each lost in contemplation. To his everlasting shame, Lucas was relieved William was not falling for Jemima, but what of the latter? Did she harbour feelings for William?

Just then, the subject of his thoughts burst into the room, bringing with her a cool draft, her cheeks glowing.

"Brrr... where on earth have you been?" Lucas suppressed a shiver, as she skidded to a halt at the opposite side of the bed from where he was sitting.

"I promised the captain a snowflake." Gingerly, she opened her hands — all but blue with cold — within which were what appeared to be white crumbs. "Hold out your hand," she entreated.

William did as she asked, whereupon Jemima tipped some of the crumbs onto his outstretched palm. Blowing softly over them, they separated and, for a brief moment a single snowflake rested on one of William's fingers.

"You too," she did the same for Lucas, and while both men felt they should scorn such frivolity, were mesmerised by the fragility of her offering.

"I know they are already melting and are better seen outside when the snow is falling, but I promised and well…"

A little embarrassed by her enthusiasm, what to her was a thing of unparalleled beauty was probably just white mush to the two soldiers, Jemima stopped talking. She reached for a cloth and handed it to William.

"You will probably need to dry your hands. I… errr… should check to see whether Isaac needs my help."

She dashed out before either man could stop her.

"What the deuce was that about?" Lucas mused, perplexed.

William chuckled. "I could hazard a guess."

Lucas raised a quizzical brow.

"Perhaps she might appreciate afternoon tea, or better still, a stroll around the park. Apparently, snow in all its forms captivates her."

Lucas stared at William in bewilderment. "Tea? A constitutional?"

"Are you forgetting our most recent discussion…" William left that dangling and, after a protracted moment, Lucas felt his heart thud.

"You think so?" He dared not hope.

"For a man of the world you are clearly an amateur when it comes to women."

"Explain yourself, man," Lucas demanded.

"Can you not see what is right in front of you?" William tsked. "I am not, and have never been, of any interest to Jemima."

"How do you—"

"I grew up among people whose whole lives are ruled by the slightest of gestures and subtlest of nuances, where the merest flicker of an eye can tell you more than half a page in a book.

Jemima studies you when she thinks no one is looking. She is not guileful enough to disguise her innermost feelings, especially to anyone wise to the art. Go and ask whether you might walk her home, or to this book shop she waxes lyrical about. You never know where it might lead."

"Yes, but—"

"No buts," William interrupted again, "just go. I shall still be here on the morrow."

He grinned, and Lucas was reminded of the last time he witnessed the carefree attitude of this engaging young soldier — it had been less than twenty four hours before the tragedy that almost took his life. William was slowly becoming... well... William again.

"Not sure how appropriate it is for a captain to order about a major, but in this instance, I'll let it pass. Rest easy, Harcourt." They shook hands and, resolution in his stride, Lucas left the room; William's amused, "invite me to the wedding," floating after him down the corridor.

Lucas made his way to the ward where he found Isaac playing chess with one of the other patients. Unhooking his overcoat from the rack, he asked the orderly whether he had seen Miss Parsons.

"Sorry, sir, she hasn't been back since she finished making this room look like some kind of botanical grotto," his resigned tone suggesting he found Jemima's determination to make the wards seasonal, bemusing yet unsurprising. "I daresay she'll be back in the morning."

Jemima had been coming long enough that she was almost part of the furniture, her presence barely noteworthy.

Lucas muttered something, shrugged into the heavy coat, and hurried from the room, down the several flights of stairs and out into the cold.

He stood for a moment staring up and down the street. *Curses*, he did not even know where she lived. *What was the name of that bookshop again?* About to dash back in to ask Jack whether he could help, he spotted a familiar figure in the distance. Jemima.

The pavement was slippery, frustrating his attempt to catch up with her, but he walked as quickly as possible. Jemima did not appear to be in a hurry. Her shoulders were hunched under her cloak and she was scuffing her feet through the snow.

To Lucas, she looked lonely in the waning light of a winter's afternoon and, seeing her on her own, caused him to ponder why she had no chaperone. A vague curiosity immediately forgotten in his haste to reach her side.

"Miss Parsons, Jemima," he called when near enough not to sound as though he was bawling her name. She either did not hear or was choosing to ignore him. He increased his pace. "Jemima, please wait."

He saw her pause, and imagined she was debating with herself whether to do as he asked. Without realising it, he held his breath.

Ahead, Jemima was in a ferment. He had followed her. She could not believe he had followed her. Half, no in truth most, of her was thrilled, but the remainder was still flustered by her behaviour over the snowflake.

She dithered, trying to decide whether she should just keep walking, even as she felt herself turn to face him, her posture rigid.

Lucas began to breathe again.

Slowing as he approached, Lucas, mildly perturbed by Jemima's odd behaviour, registered her guarded stance. Determined to break through her defences, he offered a genial smile.

"Thank you," he said cheerfully, as he reached her side.

"Is there something you want, Major?" Jemima enquired, pleased with her cool politeness. She kept her eyes on the lapels of his greatcoat, noting his chest heaving a little. This was *no* help to her composure

"If you permit, I should like to escort you home, perhaps via the park or a warm tea house, or even your favourite book shop," he replied.

Her head shot up and she held his gaze. "Why?"

"Because I enjoy your company."

"Oh." Jemima frowned. She really did not have an answer for that, so she just stared, aware of how rude it was but unable to stop herself. She shook her head. "I beg your pardon, but I—"

"Miss Parsons, please do not deny me the pleasure of taking a walk with you. Mayhap, we can have a proper conversation, who knows, we might discover we have more in common than soldiers in a hospital ward."

He smiled, encouragingly, and she capitulated, despite knowing it was probably a huge mistake, and would only make it harder when their paths no longer crossed.

He crooked his arm, and after a split second of indecision, she slipped hers through it, her gloved hand coming to rest on the dark blue of his greatcoat.

Relief flooded through Lucas when Jemima accepted his arm. After a short silence, he asked an innocuous question about books, and before long they were chatting without any awkwardness.

Jemima directed him towards The Wise Owl, saying the bookshop also served hot beverages, if he had no objection.

"As I have little idea where any of the tea houses are, save perhaps Gunther's. I will follow your lead," Lucas assured her.

Shortly thereafter, they were sitting in a bay window sipping hot coffee, discussing Jack's prognosis.

Chapter Seven

It was three days before Jemima saw Lucas again.

After enjoying two cups of coffee and a plate of tasty cakes made by Lucy, the same Lucy who set aside books for Jemima and whom the latter regarded as a good friend, Lucas walked Jemima home.

This turned out to be a narrow three-storey terraced house, far enough on the right side of Shaftesbury Avenue to be classed as respectable.

"My parents' home," she explained diffidently, as he climbed the three steps with her to the front door. As if by magic, the door swung open and an elderly gentleman greeted Jemima.

"Good afternoon, Hodge," Jemima replied, peeling off her gloves. She faced Lucas and dipped a brief curtsy. "Thank you for your kindness, Maj... Lucas. I appreciate you taking time out of your busy day."

"Kindness? I was not being kind, Jemima," his tone, a little harsh. He took a breath, and an emotion she could not place coloured his next words. "Kind was the last thing on my mind when I requested your company. I hope to see you again soon. Good day."

Grasping her now bare hand, he bowed. His lips grazed her knuckles and his fingers squeezed hers, so lightly it was scarcely a touch. Tipping his hat, he smiled a singularly sweet smile, which sent another one of those delicious frissons all the way down Jemima's spine, and strode away.

She watched him walk down the street, turn the corner and vanish out of sight. He was so tall, yet every movement was efficient, not an ounce of energy wasted. She supposed that was a military thing.

His eyes — not quite blue, more they were reminiscent of that moment when dusk becomes night, a sort of inky purple — seemed watchful and maybe a little wary. His features were... what was the word...? craggy? He was not handsome in the traditional sense, but there was something.

She pondered this for a few moments until Hodge coughed, and suggested she come inside, or she would catch her death.

While eating her evening meal in isolated splendour in the snug dining room, a fire crackling merrily in the grate, it came to Jemima, her fork half-way to her mouth.

Arresting.

That was it, he was arresting. An indefinable characteristic really, and one which pertained to each individual beholder not the subject. What *she* saw would not be what anyone else saw and, like a bolt from the blue, she realised she did not want another woman to *see* Lucas at all. She might steal him away.

Goodness gracious, Jemima, she chastised herself, *he is not yours*.

With deliberation, her fingers trembling, she placed her cutlery neatly on the plate. A delicate pink warmed her cheeks as several random moments, emotions, and sensations collided.

"Well, bloody hell," she bit down on the crude expletive, stunned it had taken her so long to recognise what, now she accepted it, had been patently obvious for some time. "I do not even know him? How is this possible?" Unknowingly echoing Lucas' thoughts of earlier that day.

Shy of facing Lucas, certain her feelings would be clear for all to see, Jemima found other distractions to keep her occupied for a couple of days. To little avail. She missed him, a sentiment she found hard to fathom because she had never 'had him' to miss… her rather convoluted internal discussion only serving to baffle her further.

Thus, and somewhat reluctantly, she set off for St Bart's at her usual time the following morning.

Her stomach was tied in knots by the time she arrived at the hospital. So distracted was she, that eventually, after she had tripped over a chair, dropped a tray of bandages, and spilt coffee over two of the broadsheets, Isaac was moved to ask whether she was quite well.

"My apologies, Isaac. My coordination seems a little awry this morning. I cannot think what is wrong with me."

Unbidden, Isaac recalled a curious request what was it, two, three days ago and swallowed a chuckle. He had two sisters, and surmised he might know the root of the problem. Still, Jemima was no use to anyone while her concentration was elsewhere.

"Why don't you go and read to Captain Harcourt? I doubt you can cause any damage doing that," he suggested wryly.

"Yes, yes, I shall, good idea," Jemima replied distractedly. She selected a couple of books from the pile and meandered slowly to William's quiet room. Knocking softly, she pushed open the door, to find Lucas already there, the two men embroiled in what looked like a deep discussion.

They looked up at her entrance, and William smiled. Her gaze fell on Lucas, whose expression remained bland, indifferent almost.

No indication he had come to find her down a snowy street, walked her to a tea shop, and then all the way home. This man who had kissed her hand and squeezed her fingers, who had smiled that heart-stopping smile.

Her brow creased. *Had she imagined it? Oh God, when he said the last thing, he was being was kind, had he meant he was with her out of some misguided sense of duty? Was it all because of Jack?*

Hot colour flared up her cheeks, and she wanted to wake up to find this day, the whole darn lot of it was naught but a bad dream.

She was unaware the two books had slipped out of her nerveless fingers, hitting the floor with a dull thud. "S-sorry… errr… maybe… I'll…" she stammered, and backed out, shaking her head at her own capricious behaviour.

Honestly, she was being ridiculous. Get a hold of yourself, Jemima. You are a grown woman, do try to act like one.

"Jemi—"

She did not hear the rest of her name as the door swung closed. Fighting a childish urge to cry, she all but ran down the corridor.

Angry with herself for letting her emotions overwhelm her, she did not bother returning to the ward, neither did she remember to collect her cloak. She fled down the stairs and out into the frigid morning.

Lucas was held motionless after Jemima's precipitous departure. *What had just happened?* It was only when William nudged him that he refocused on his surroundings.

"You need to tell her. If you don't, either this nonsense will keep happening, or you will never see her again."

"Huh?" Still confounded.

"Withers, go. She looked like everything was falling in on her. I expect the poor girl only just recognised she's in love with you, and fears looking like a fool if her feelings are not reciprocated."

"How could you possibly know that?" Lucas demanded, his head spinning. *She loved him? Was there any chance?*

"Because I am very wise." William grinned. "Tell her I said hello." The mundanity of the comment tugged the hint of a smile from Lucas' lips.

"Maybe I ought to be promoted to Major," William ruminated. "For a man now working in a covert capacity, you seem markedly… unobservant. I may have to advise your supervisors, I am concerned you are losing your edge."

"Insubordination will not be tolerated, *Captain* Harcourt." Lucas laughed, suddenly light of heart. "I wonder whether a Christmas wedding is too soon?"

William groaned. "You have to find her first but, if Jemima is addled enough to want to marry you, get her down the aisle before she comes to her senses. Oh, and please pass me those books before you go dashing after her."

Chapter Eight

Jemima was cursing her contrary brain. Not only had she overreacted to a situation that did not warrant such an extreme response but also, she had left her cloak hanging on the rack in the main ward. *Dammit!*

That said, she did have her wrap and was absolutely determined not to retrace her steps, knowing there was every likelihood she would run into Lucas.

Her erratic conduct would doubtless quash any admiration he might have begun to feel. *She was such an idiot. She ought to offer lessons in how* not *to present oneself as poised and mature — the way she was behaving at the moment she would be rich as Croesus in no time.*

Jemima groaned. Then there was Jack. Why, oh why, did Lucas have to be his commanding officer? What a mess; one she had no intention of dealing with today. Today, she was going home to hide from the world, and pretend she had never got out of bed.

Shivering in the freezing air, she rummaged in the hidden pocket of her skirts to see whether she had any coin for a hackney. Withdrawing one miserable farthing, her heart sank; that was not enough to get her home. While she vacillated, snow began to drift down from a heavy sky, and the breeze sharpened.

She needed to get home — and quickly. Glancing around, she spotted the gate to the park. It didn't really shorten her journey by much, but was far preferable to tramping along muddy streets, while avoiding spray from carriage wheels.

Contorting her lovely features into a fearful grimace, worthy of one of the witches in the fairy tales she loved to read, Jemima headed to the park.

It was barely five minutes between Jemima's hasty exit from William's room, and Lucas' rather more measured one. He assumed she had gone along to see Jack, and thus did not hurry. Upon entering the ward, he spotted Jack, sitting by the fire, his leg up on a chair, reading a broadsheet.

"Morning, Private. Have you seen Jemima?" Lucas greeted him.

"No, sir, she was here earlier, but Isaac sent her to read to Cap'n Harcourt, she was all fingers and thumbs." Jack paused, and actually looked at Lucas properly.

Something flitted through his mind. A couple of comments Jemima had made, her expression when anyone mentioned the major's name. Jack was not particularly interested in or sensitive to the vagaries of romance, but he loved his sister and, suddenly, two and two added up to about ten. He glowered at Lucas.

"Might you know why… errr… sir?" Jack frowned, his tones not quite as deferential as they ought to be, but at least he remembered who he was addressing.

"Possibly, maybe, I hope so," Lucas replied, not very coherently. He heaved a sigh and pulled up a chair. "Jack, I know this is not a subject easily discussed, but might I ask whether Jemima has a suitor?"

The unexpected query, along with relief his superior was not playing games with his sister, elicited an irreverent bark of laughter.

"Jemima, a suitor? Oh, sir." Jack rocked with mirth at the very idea, eventually sobering enough to explain that no, Jemima was not being courted, as far as he knew. She was much too stubborn and wilful to relinquish her hard won, and still limited, independence.

"When Papa died, Mama just gave up, and Jem had no alternative but to shoulder the responsibilities of a household. She organised the funeral, took care of Mama, me, and the domestic staff. Papa was a solicitor, a successful one, and although we are not wealthy, he was astute enough to ensure we would not go without.

"Nevertheless, Jem had to learn how to apportion finances across wages, food, wood for the fires, and so on. Which merchants and tradespeople were trustworthy. For a while every time I came home, she was buried in accounts.

"Without Papa, Mama lost the will to live, and died less than a year later. Jem never complains, but I think she might be tired, and her irascibility comes from being worried she is somehow letting us, the staff and me, down."

It was a long speech from the young man, surprising Jack, as well as Lucas who, of course, had no idea about the Parsons' private life. That his commanding officer might have developed an affection for Jemima sat well with Jack, but he remained somewhat confused.

"Were you hoping to speak with Jemima?" Remembering Lucas' earlier question.

"Dash it all, yes. She… I… errm…" Lucas gave Jack the barest details of *that* afternoon. While he was talking, his words when he left her doorstep, came back to him, and he realised Jemima might have misunderstood his meaning.

"Oh, now I see why..." he did not elaborate, and instead said, distractedly, "excuse me, I have to go."

Jack watched Lucas hurry along the ward, a wry smile forming as he rolled the major's comments around in his head. Turning back to the broadsheet, he was soon immersed in all things political, and all but forgot their conversation.

Lucas could not get the words out of his head. He had told her kind was the last thing he was being. *How the hell had she misconstrued that?*

Shrugging into his greatcoat, he was about to reach for his hat, when he spotted a lady's cloak hanging on one of the other hooks. His hand brushed against the fine wool and a familiar scent wafted past his nose. Jemima. It was Jemima's cloak.

He looked out of the window and saw it was snowing steadily. How could one forget to take a coat in this weather? He shook his head. Ramming his hat on, and pulling on a pair of thick gloves, Lucas grabbed the cloak, and left the ward. Taking the stairs two at a time, he was outside in seconds.

Scanning the street, Lucas tried to work out which direction Jemima might take. As his eyes roved the street, he spotted the gate at the far end, leading to the park. *Would she go that way?*

A carriage rattled by, slush mixed with tiny chunks of gravel sprayed up from the road and he had his answer. Setting a brisk pace, he attempted to catch up to the woman who, without even trying, had stolen his heart.

Chapter Nine

It was bitterly cold, and the snow was becoming heavier. Jemima was sure she ought to be at the other side of the park by now. It wasn't that big. It must be at least ten minutes since she entered.

Huffing a frustrated sigh, she stopped and tried to orient herself, spying what looked like a large, dead tree branch at the side of the path. She peered at it, pursing her lips. *Hadn't she already walked passed that? How was it possible to walk in circles in a park barely the size of a garden?*

Jemima growled one of Jack's favourite expletives and kicked viciously at the branch. Huge, great big, enormous mistake. The branch might be dead, but it was solid. Pain jarred her toes and shot up her leg, making her eyes water and, when she tried to put any weight on her foot, it was agony.

Just great.

Hobbling to a wrought iron bench at the edge of the path, Jemima brushed off the snow as best she could and slumped down, contemplating her misfortune. *Could this day get any worse?* she grumbled inwardly.

Her foot throbbed, she was cold, she was miserable, she had

made a complete ninny of herself, and was doubtless going to catch a cold from being silly enough to forget her cloak.

She huddled into her wrap, which although relatively thick, was not enough to prevent the damp from seeping through.

Without warning, everything crowded in. Not least being the fact, she had gone and fallen in love with a most irritating gentleman, but one in whose gaze she could quite happily drown. Whose touch she yearned to feel again, and whose smile made her feel safe, protected, and, oddly, remembering the afternoon he walked her home, adored.

"This weather is getting to my head," she groused to the empty park. Hoping if she sat for a few more minutes, the pain in her foot might ease to a point where she could walk home, Jemima leaned back, closed her eyes, and took several deep breaths.

Lucas marched into the park, eyes searching. No sign of Jemima. If he hadn't spotted her by the time he reached the gate at the far side, he would assume she had taken a hackney and was already home. It wouldn't take long for him to hail one of his own.

He wanted to check on her well-being, if only to be assured she had come to no harm. His reason for calling, easily explained, was to return her cloak — at least, that was what he kept telling himself.

He rounded a bend in the path and his heart nearly jumped out of his chest. There on a bench, head back, was Jemima. Abject relief made him a bit giddy and his stride quickened.

"Jemima," he called her name and saw her turn in his direction. Even from several feet away he noticed her pinched lips and pallid cheeks. *Something was badly wrong.*

"Jemima?" Hastily, he closed the gap.

. . .

Jemima heard his voice and, for a split second, thought she had fallen asleep and was dreaming. Opening her eyes, she sat up and glanced towards the sound. It *was* him.

"L-Lucas?" Even to Jemima she sounded strained and, without thinking, she jumped up off the bench. Her sore foot landed hard on the stone footpath.

Pain lanced through her, and black spots danced in her vision. Nausea threatened, and she was unable to prevent an agonised scream while everything began to recede. No, she would *not* faint, she would not fa…

She had no idea Lucas caught her before she crumpled to the ground.

"I've got you, my love," he said, even knowing she would not hear. Glancing down at the woman in his arms, he felt a wave of emotion slam into him with such force it almost knocked him off his feet too, and that would *not* do.

Steadying himself, he sat down on the same bench and tucked Jemima's cloak around her shoulders. Rubbing her arms and hands to get some heat into them, he pondered whether it would be quicker to return to the hospital or keep going and hope to flag down a passing hackney.

He opted for the latter. After a minute or so, he stood, Jemima in his arms, and made his way through the park. He was a tad confused as to why she had only gone so short a distance, but that was a discussion for another time. Right now, the most important thing was to warm her up, get her home, and probably summon a doctor.

"Come on, sweetheart, you are home, and we need to get you inside, out of the cold," a voice, full of gentle tenderness coaxed her from the blessed darkness.

She murmured a negative and shifted to get more comfortable against the cushion.

"Jemima. Please, my love, we cannot sit in this carriage all day."

My love... carriage... what now? She shot up, almost falling off whatever she was sitting on in her haste. A strong arm held her, averting an ignominious bump on the floor of the carriage.

Twisting, Jemima came face-to-face with Lucas. His midnight blue eyes studying her, brow creased in concern. Taking in her surroundings, she noted she was on his knee. Her cheeks flushed a delicate pink, but she could not tear away her gaze.

He really was the most handsome man she had ever laid eyes on. Such deep blue eyes, they twinkled — she swore they twinkled, and his lips... *oh, goodness gracious, they were sinfully sensual.* Just as she was imagining what he could do with those lips, she registered that what she assumed to be a cushion must have been Lucas.

The pink became fiery red.

"I do not think you ought to put your foot down, but if you permit, I will assist you into your home." His voice penetrated her embarrassment, his tones persuasive.

Incapable of replying, she nodded, her mouth felt as though someone had stuffed it full of snow.

Lucas slid Jemima onto the carriage seat and, careful not to bang her foot, opened the door, hopped down, and crossed the path. She heard the click of the front gate and the metallic rap of the door knocker. A moment's silence, then the rumble of conversation.

Two faces appeared at the carriage door.

"Good afternoon, Hodge." Jemima tried to smile, but it was beyond her.

"Good afternoon, Miss Parsons. The Major 'ere says you've 'urt your foot."

"Allow me," Lucas interposed. He climbed inside the carriage, lifted Jemima as though she weighed no more than a feather pillow and, aided by Hodge, stepped back onto the pavement.

Hodge led the way through the door, and along the hall to the parlour, where a fire burned merrily in a large grate, and several candelabra were lit, casting a cosy glow around the room.

"A bowl of warm water, a blanket, and maybe send someone for the doctor. Miss Parsons' foot should be examined properly." Lucas threw out his instructions, expecting them to be carried out with the same military efficiency as would any soldier under his command.

"Please," Jemima added, grasping Hodge's arm when he turned to do as he was bidden.

Hodge patted her shoulder. "Fret not, Miss. I'll send Thad. He'll be back with Doctor Simpson forthwith."

As the faithful retainer left the room, Jemima fidgeted in her chair, trying to think of some witty remark, some insightful repartee. All she could come up with was, "Thank you."

"You are most welcome." Lucas hesitated, then continued. "Jemima…"

Whatever he was about to say was lost because right at that moment, Lizzy and Mrs Hodge bustled in. Between them they carried a soft blanket, a basket of cloths and lotions, as well as two hot coffees, a plate of freshly baked biscuits, and the requested bowl of warm water.

"Here you are, my lovely," Mrs Hodge said as she placed every-thing within easy reach. "Just ring if you need anything else." She did not leave. It was not her place to interfere, but she did not know this gentleman, and Miss Parsons, well, she was unmarried. It wasn't right.

Inwardly frustrated, *what was Lucas about to say?* Jemima nevertheless maintained her customary courtesy. "Mrs Hodge, may I introduce Major Lucas Withers, Jack's commanding officer and the man who was kind enough to bring me home. We have... errr... become acquainted in the last few weeks."

She did not feel it necessary to justify his presence but felt that pink stain wash up her cheeks again.

Sensing they were being, albeit very politely, dismissed, Mrs Hodge nodded briskly, while Lizzy dipped a curtsy, and the pair left the room.

"You were saying?" Jemima stared at Lucas, holding his gaze, willing him to tell her what she hoped had not been her vivid imagination conjuring up something from nothing.

Chapter Ten

Lucas returned her gaze with interest. He watched her beautiful eyes study him, and discerned trepidation in their hazel depths. His heart, beating a tattoo worthy of a drum-major, pounded so loudly in his chest he was surprised she made no comment.

"Jemima. I am but a simple soldier, practical of mind and logical of thought. I struggle to find the words I need to say, to help you understand how I feel. I presumed my intent was clear the day we shared tea at The Wise Owl, but this morning, when I was talking to Jack—"

"You talked to Jack?" Jemima interrupted, narrowing her eyes.

"I was looking for you and thought you might be with your brother."

Jemima smiled then, a delicious sensation beginning to coil around her centre. "You were looking for me? Why, Lucas?"

Lucas searched her face. A face which had been meddling with his mind since first he laid eyes on it. What was the point of trying to couch his intent in flowery words and gestures? Yes, Jemima deserved to be romanced, but this needed to be unequivocal and thus, unembellished would be better.

"Jemima, I love you," he said baldly. "I think I have been in love with you almost since the day we met, when you chastised me for sending Jack into battle. When I said kind was the last thing I was being, it was naught to do with Jack or William, or St Bart's, it was because I wanted to be with *you*. Jemima, I want to hold your hand, kiss your enticing lips, enfold you in my arms and never let you go. Is there any hope you might come to have an affection for me? If not, please, tell me straight. I—"

A soft knock and the door opened to admit Hodge and Doctor Simpson.

Oh, these confounded interruptions. Jemima nearly screamed again. This time it was nothing to do with her foot, the pain of which had taken second place to the tumult in her head. He loved her. *Be still my beating heart.* Ignoring the doctor, Jemima reached across the gap between the chairs.

"Miss—" Hodge started to say.

"Shhh…" she hissed, gesticulating wildly, effectively hushing the speaker, uncaring that this was the height of rudeness. "This is important. Please, say that again," she entreated the man whose hand she now grasped.

"Tell me straight…" his lips beginning to curve in a wicked smile.

"No, silly, not that bit, the first bit."

Lucas did not hesitate. "I love you, Jemima."

A beam, radiant enough to light the whole of St Bart's lit Jemima's face. "You do?"

"With all my heart."

Not willing to risk another fainting spell by standing, she gripped his fingers tightly, using them as leverage to lean over and place a chaste kiss on his cheek. Lucas moved at the last second and the air whooshed out of her lungs when he brushed her lips with his.

Unutterable joy began to spiral through her and, to the well-concealed amusement of Hodge and the doctor, Jemima announced, clear as a bell.

"I love you too."

Much later, after Dr Simpson was eventually allowed to examine Jemima's foot — pronouncing badly bruised toes, of which two were probably broken, and prescribing a few days rest — Jemima and Lucas were finally alone.

Mrs Hodges intimated, delicately, that Lizzy ought to act as chaperone, a suggestion rejected with as much tact as Jemima was able to summon up.

A light lunch was served in the parlour, at Jemima's request. She was unable to countenance the thought of walking anywhere unless she absolutely had to, and there they remained.

It was a warm and cosy room. Furniture chosen for comfort not to demonstrate status. The decor was simple. Curtains and upholstery were of quiet, muted hues, brightened here and there by the splashes of colour in the rich red rug, the cushions, and the minimal ornaments; the combination creating a tranquil space.

Outside the snow continued to fall, and though only mid-afternoon it was almost dark outside; the thick blanket of white obscuring the city, not enough to alleviate the gloom. While they were sipping steaming hot chocolate, and chatting about upcoming winter events, Jemima's mind was working overtime.

What she was about to suggest was unorthodox in the extreme, but she was prepared to take the chance. When there was a suitable break in their conversation, she launched in.

"Lucas, I am inclined to propose you stay here tonight. We have plenty of guest chambers already made up. I do not want you walking home in this blizzard." Holding her breath at her audacity.

Startled, Lucas counted to ten before answering, wholly cognisant of what Jemima risked by such a request. "I should have no trouble getting home, my love. Moreover, I have no desire to besmirch your reputation by flouting convention."

"Pooh to that," was her considered response. "I do not suppose anyone will be aware of your presence, save my household and they know better than to gossip. Do stay," she repeated, blissfully unaware of the effect of her smile.

Lucas' eminently sensible arguments dwindled with the daylight.

"I admit your offer is tempting. Not to venture forth on so inclement an evening sounds inviting but being in such close proximity might prove my undoing." He made a half-hearted attempt to dissuade her.

Silently cursing her sore foot, Jemima placed her cup on the little table between their chairs, and stretched out her hand, delight rippling through her when his large hand engulfed her much smaller one. Gingerly, she stood, and tugged on his fingers.

In quick understanding, Lucas got to his feet.

"I am of the opinion, you ought to demonstrate precisely what you mean." She grinned impishly, two fingers tracking over his waistcoat, fiddling with the buttons — Lucas had shed his jacket earlier, at Jemima's insistence.

"Are you seducing me, Miss Parsons?"

"Do you object?"

"Not in the slightest." Bending his head, he captured her lips with his.

The moment their mouths met, Jemima lost all capacity to think. His lips were gentle — teasing, tasting. If this wasn't distraction enough, his hands began stroking over her slender frame, tracing her shape as though imprinting it into his fingertips.

Her first real kiss, goodness me, it was utterly sublime.

Needing to touch him, her hands stole up his arms to his broad shoulders. Sliding around his neck, to entangle themselves in the silky blackness of his hair.

His arms tightened around her. Jemima could feel the throb of his heart against her breast, and the warmth of his lips as he kissed a heated path down her throat. Her breathing quickened, and when he reached the sensitive hollow at the base of her neck, her head fell back exposing her décolletage.

Lucas groaned, the sight setting his blood on fire. Surrendering to his baser instincts for one more moment, he let his lips drift over her silken skin, dipping to the rise of her breast. Before his passion spiralled out of control, he cradled her head and brought his mouth back to hers.

Eventually, the did come up for air, both panting slightly, eyes glassy, and Jemima's hair was delightfully mussed. To Lucas, she was the most enchanting vision.

"Jemima, we must stop, or your brother will be obliged to call me out, which will not look good on my record," his voice was husky with desire and just a hint of wry humour.

"Must we?" Jemima stroked a trembling finger along his jawline, her head spinning.

"For now, however," he paused, scouring his brain for the perfect way to phrase what he wanted to say, "maybe we do not have to wait too much longer."

His arms still around her, Jemima leaned back a little, in order to read his expression. A crease began to form on her brow, so he kissed it, just because he could.

"Jemima Parsons…" he kissed the tip of her nose, "…would you do me the greatest honour," he kissed her oh so inviting lips, "of agreeing to become my wife?"

Chapter Eleven

Jemima's mouth fell open in shock. "Wh... bu... if... did..." she swallowed and closed her eyes briefly, trying to corral her chaotic thoughts.

A total waste of time because Lucas kissed her eyelids.

How was she supposed to think clearly?

"You're not," she heard him murmur next to her ear.

"I beg your pardon."

"You're not supposed to think clearly, you're supposed to think with glorious, delectable, dizzying, confusion and with your heart..."

Dammit, she said that out loud?

"Yes, you did?" Kissing her again.

"Lucas," she chided, gently.

"Yes, my love," he sounded wholly unrepentant.

"I cannot possibly give your proposal serious deliberation if you keep kissing me."

"That is rather the point. 'Tis a deliberate tactic. One we often employed during the war, to great effect, on any we suspected of being a spy."

Jemima gaped, only to burst out laughing at his salacious expression.

"Hmmm… I do not believe I shall succumb to your shameless methods." One finger resting on her chin contemplatively.

"Might I be so bold as to submit for your approval, another method which has proven successful?" His gaze nothing short of smouldering

"Errr… mmm…" Jemima squeaked in shock when Lucas, giving her no chance to refuse, swung her into his arms and carried her across the room to the chaise.

Once seated, he settled her on his lap, cupped her head in both hands and kissed her until she thought she might faint all over again.

"Luc… Luc… oh." She gave up and sank into the multitude of sensations coursing through her. Of their own volition, her fingers reached for and untied his cravat, flinging it with little care, somewhere over her shoulder.

Next, she turned her attention to the buttons on his waistcoat which fell like soldiers under fire to her persistence. Yanking at the soft cotton of his shirt, she was gratified to hear him hiss when her hands came into contact with his warm flesh.

"Jemima," he rasped, "wha… urrrgghhhhh." Her cool fingertips brushed over his chest, undermining his resolve. Good job this was *not* an interrogation. One arm around her back, Lucas slid his other hand down to the hem of her skirt, taking care not to jar her foot.

Seeking under layers of fine wool and linen, his hand began a tortuously slow glide up her stocking-clad leg.

He stopped at her calf and felt her shudder.

"Marry me, Jemima."

"We…ll," she drew out the word.

He reached her knee, fingertips circling the bone, teasing the tender spot at the back of the joint.

"Marry me, Jemima."

Jemima was enjoying the game, and wanted to test his mettle, to see how far he would take it.

A fire kindled in her core. Instinctively, she knew Lucas was the only one to douse the flames or, and better still, to stoke them until they became a conflagration.

"I need more t-time to p-ponder," stammering when his hand ghosted higher.

"Marry me."

His mouth grazed her ear lobe, at the same moment as languid fingertips skimmed the soft skin at the top of her thigh, above her stocking, and she bit her lip to stop from moaning.

Goodness, but she was a brazen chit. A soft whimper slipped out when his relentless fingers found their goal.

"Lucas," she gasped, twisting in his embrace, the better to hold his gaze, aware she was poised on the brink of something astonishing.

"Marry me, Jemima."

"What will you do if I cannot decide?"

"Withdraw my hand."

"Do not dare."

"Then say yes." His fingers nudged her, sparking *the* most incredible sensation, making her inch closer, and sending her heart rate soaring.

"You are not playing fair."

"I never had any intention of playing fair. I love you, I want you. Marry me, Jemima." He stroked her, and she all but flipped off his lap, only his arm around her held her steady.

"…and if I say yes…" she managed, hoarsely

"I will quench the fire."

Jemima stared into his eyes which reflected the flicker of the candles, their midnight depths mesmerising. Her heart swelled.

"Yes." The word coasted on a sigh, which quickly turned into the moan she had tried so hard not to utter.

. . .

Lucas did not renege on his promise.

The snow continued to fall, although not quite as heavily and, by the end of the following week, the clouds had cleared, allowing a pale, wintry sun to break through.

Lucas and Jemima shared their happy news with their nearest and dearest, which turned out to be less than a dozen people, but whose congratulations were heartfelt and enthusiastic.

Jemima's foot healed, too slowly for Jemima's liking, but Lucas ensured she did not overdo it. Planning their wedding proved diversion enough to keep her sitting down for much of the day.

Jack begged to be discharged before their nuptials and had already asked Jemima whether he might stand in the stead of their father. Dr Latham, pleased with Private Parsons' progress was happy to release the young man, on the strict proviso, he agreed to have his injury checked by his own doctor on a regular basis, until completely healed.

William also escaped the confines of St Bart's for a week over the Christmas period, glad to be sleeping in the comfort of his own bed, albeit briefly. His meagre staff welcomed him back to Harcourt House, their joy at his return evidenced in the festive atmosphere they had created in the habitually silent and rather bleak home, to the amazement and quiet appreciation of their master.

Two days before Christmas, three weeks after he proposed, Lucas and Jemima were wed. A simple yet reverent service, after which

William generously hosted a sumptuous wedding breakfast for the guests, at his home.

The day was full of merriment, but as the afternoon waned, the happy couple slipped away unnoticed. Unbeknownst to his new wife, Lucas had arranged for leave, allowing them to take a short holiday, and they would be departing early on the morrow.

William had offered them the use of Blackthorne Manor, nestled in the countryside half a day's ride from London, and Lucas did not want to risk being delayed by the weather. It was modest, William said, but would give them some privacy, and the grounds were large enough to get lost in, should they be so inspired.

Moreover, Lucas was finding it torment to keep his hands off Jemima. Everything about her beguiled him, and for someone who, less than two months ago could not have imagined anyone ensnaring him so completely, he relinquished his autonomy happily.

As they stepped down from the carriage, the snow began to fall again; light flakes spiralling down from the leaden sky. Lucas was reminded of a conversation he overheard not so very long ago, prompting him to pause at their gate.

Lifting his gloved hand, palm up, he waited until several of the delicate wisps settled before speaking, the rich timbre of his voice surrounding Jemima, like an embrace.

"Jemima, my beautiful wife, recently you told a grievously injured soldier that snowflakes are like minuscule pieces of the most fragile lace, made from cobwebs. That each one is different, and if lucky enough to catch one, to see its exquisite delicacy before it melts, it is like a gift from God."

Startled, Jemima stared up at him, her eyes glistening. "I had no idea you heard me say that."

"I did not wish to interrupt, but that was the moment I fell in love with you, although my head was not quite ready to accept my heart's choice. Like a snowflake, you are exquisite, delicate, and very precious, as well as — and maybe rather less like a snowflake — spirited, tenacious, and headstrong. You are indeed one of a kind, and I thank my lucky stars that when you tumbled into my life like a miniature blizzard, I was smart enough to catch you."

A radiant smile lit Jemima's face. "Lucas, my darling husband, that is one of the most wonderful things anyone has ever said to me. I love you too and am so glad yours were the arms into which I fell." She stretched up, slid her hands around his neck, and, uncaring that they were in the middle of the street, and anyone might see them, kissed him into insensibility.

The snow whirled around them and Lucas, concerned they would soon resemble snowmen, swung his wife into his arms and planted a kiss on her cold nose — responding to her shocked squeak by telling her they *were* newly-weds, making his gesture entirely appropriate.

Then, he carried her inside and up the stairs to their bedchamber, where he spent quite some considerable time illustrating just how precious she was.

Christmas 1814 was white and cold but, for Jemima and Lucas, it was absolutely perfect!

About the Author

Rosie Chapel lives in Perth, Australia with her hubby and three furkids. When not writing, she loves catching up with friends, burying herself in a book (or three), discovering the wonders of Western Australia, or — and the best — a quiet evening at home with her husband, enjoying a glass of wine and a movie.

Website: https://rosiechapel.com/

Also by Rosie Chapel

The Linen and Lace Series

Once Upon An Earl - Book One

To Unlock Her Heart - Book Two

Love on a Winter's Tide - Book Three

A Love Unquenchable - Book Four

A Hidden Rose — Book Five

The Daffodil Garden

The Unconventional Duchess

Rescuing Her Knight - *the de Wiltons:* Book One

Elusive Hearts - *An Unexpected Romance*: Book One

His Fiery Hoyden

A Regency Duet

A Regency Christmas Double

Fate is Curious

A Christmas Prayer *with Ashlee Shades*

The Lady's Wager

Winning Emma

A Love Impossible

Unravelling Roana

Love Kindled

Moonbeams and Mistletoe

Fairy Tale Romance

Chasing Bluebells

Contemporary Romances

Of Ruins and Romance

All At Once It's You

Cobweb Dreams

Just One Step

His Heart's Second Sigh

<u>Dystopian Romance</u>

Echoes & Illusions *with Rori Bleu*

Historical Fiction/Romance

The Pomegranate Tree
Hannah's Heirloom - Book One

Hoping to trace the origins of an ancient ruby clasp, a gift from her long dead grandmother, Hannah Wilson travels to the fortress of Masada with her best friend, Max. Strange dreams concerning a rebel ambush begin to haunt Hannah and following a tragic accident, she slips into the world of Ancient Masada.

A woman out of time, Hannah must rely on her instincts and her knowledge of what will befall this citadel to survive. Will she escape, or is she doomed to die along with hundreds of others as Masada falls — and what does any of this have to do with an ancient ruby clasp?

Echoes of Stone and Fire
Hannah's Heirloom - Book Two

Pompeii - a vibrant city lost in time following the AD79 eruption of Vesuvius. Now rediscovered, archaeologists yearn for an opportunity to uncover the town's past. Some things, however, are best left alone - revealing the secrets hidden beneath the stones could prove perilous. Hannah and Max are brought to Pompeii by a surprise invitation to join an excavation team who are trying to uncover the city's long history.

After entering an excavated house that bears a Hebrew inscription, Hannah's two worlds collide, and she falls back through time to ancient Pompeii. A place where her ancestor is a physician to gladiators engaged in mortal combat, where riotous mobs run amok and where a ghost from the past returns to haunt her.

Will Hannah and her loved ones manage to escape the devastation she knows is coming, before the town is engulfed in volcanic ash? Will she ever find her way back to Max the love of her life, waiting not so patiently millennia away? Or will echoes be all that remain?

Embers of Destiny

Hannah's Heirloom - Book Three

AD80 - Hannah and Maxentius must embark on a new journey to Northern Britannia. This harsh frontier is far from the comforts of Rome and danger lurks where least expected; a garrison of soldiers, some unhappy with their isolated posting; local tribes, outwardly accepting of their Roman occupier, but who may still resent the seizure of their lands.

Millennia away, Hannah Vallier finds a familiar item while working in a museum near Hadrian's Wall. It is the pomegranate; carved by Maxentius on Masada. Before Hannah can discuss it with Max, disaster strikes! Believing her husband has been killed, Hannah retreats into the past, her soul melding with that of her ancestor, but with little idea of what they could face. Is the risk from the conquered tribes, or much closer to home?

As rebellion threatens to shatter a fragile peace, Hannah's heart whispers that just maybe Max isn't dead and that he is calling her home. Can she trust her heart, or will she remain caught out of time, her destiny floating away like embers on a breeze?

Etched in Starlight

Hannah's Heirloom - Prequel

Maxentius - a Roman soldier fresh from the battlefields of Armenia, arrives to take command of the military outpost of Masada, Herod's isolated citadel in the Judaean desert. A seemingly mundane posting after years of warfare, Maxentius finds it more challenging to maintain a focused garrison than to face the wrath of the Parthians across a disputed frontier.

Hannah - a young Hebrew physician spends her days dealing with injuries from street brawls, deprivation, disease and loss. As her beloved Jerusalem plunges into chaos, her brother — who belongs to a band of rebels determined to drive out their Roman occupiers — tells her of their plans to storm a desert fortress and steal the weapons stored there, persuading his reluctant sister to go with him.

Masada - following the ambush, Hannah finds and treats three badly wounded Roman soldiers. In the aftermath and against impossible odds, Hannah and Maxentius realise that they are more than healer and captive, their fate already etched in starlight.

Prelude to Fate

For Lucia, staring into the jaws of an horrific death, escape seems impossible.

Rufius Atellus, a veteran Roman soldier, is appalled when he recognises one of the victims about to be executed. Surely this is a ghastly mistake?

A ferocious she-wolf, anticipating a tasty meal, suddenly finds herself under a human's control.

In an unexpected twist, and as danger threatens, the lives of all three become inextricably entwined.

Was it chance brought them together in that theatre of bloodshed, or simply a prelude to fate?

Legacy of Flame and Ash

A Hannah's Heirloom Story

An unremarkable family ring — lost when its owner was killed in the catastrophic eruption of Vesuvius — is excavated after nearly two millennia buried under tons of pumice and ash, setting off an extraordinary sequence of events.

A brazen robbery, and the ring is lost again. The theft and subsequent investigation, inspire twelve-year-old Cristiano Rossi to dedicate his life to the search and recovery of stolen artefacts.

Fast forward twenty years. Whispers of a rare item being offered for sale on the black market, initiates a joint operation between the Italian and British branches of the, colloquially named, Art Squad.

Hannah Vallier and her tech savvy assistant, Bryony Emerson — whose abilities to track down the untraceable, led to them assisting the UK Art and Antiquities Unit — have unearthed an intriguing thread. Reluctantly, Cristiano agrees to team up with the pair to thwart the traffickers, retrieve the artefact and, hopefully, dismantle the site.

What ought to be a routine assignment is complicated by a rogue operative, an unexpected romance, an ancient connection, and a *very* angry ghost!

A Guardian Unexpected

The Nettleby Trilogy: Book One

August 1914: Europe is on the brink of catastrophe. In a small village in rural Lincolnshire, a wife kisses her husband goodbye.

Childhood sweethearts, Eliza and Joe have only been married two years. They could not have imagined how soon they would be torn apart by war, nor that the most unexpected of guardians would offer them hope during their darkest hours.

Under the Clock

The Nettleby Trilogy: Book Two

England 1908: Under the clock, on a sleepy station platform nestled in rural Lincolnshire, an unexpected romance blossoms.

Maisie: Every Friday, at precisely five to six, a handsome young man arrives at the station. I know the time because I can see the clock. The train pulls in, punctual as always, and among the alighting passengers is an elderly gentleman. The young man greets him with a smile and a handshake, then tucks his arm through the older man's and they leave the platform.

Every Friday.

Occasionally, we exchange a glance or two and, to be fair, I suspect I notice him more than he notices me.

Fred: I count the hours until Friday afternoon comes around. Not only because this marks the start of the weekend but also, and more importantly, I get to see the flower girl. I am clueless as to her name, yet my heart begins to race the minute the station comes into view. I almost run up the steps onto the platform, hoping for a glimpse of her bright smile.

Every Friday.

I doubt she ever notices me. I'm just a village lad, one more faceless person in the throng.

Then again, you never know what might happen… in an innocuous corner of a quiet platform…

…under the clock

Evie's War

with Rori Bleu

World War II catapulted ordinary people into extraordinary service to save the world from an insidious evil… even if that meant being forced to do things which, under normal circumstances, would be considered abhorrent.

Genevieve Rousseau, Evie to a select few, was one such person who could not escape this fate. Despite her covert endeavours to liberate Paris from the Germans, she finds herself labelled a collaborator and an enemy of the French Republic.

Her only hope of vindication lies in helping a dangerously handsome American, with questionable motives, to uncover the Germans' final revenge.

Could struggling to resist Major Jack Donovon prove to be the decisive battle in Evie's War?

Vindicta

with Rori Bleu

Nightmares come in many guises… but usually fade with the dawn…

Not so for Bobbi Jo Fletcher. A witness to the massacre of her family, she had to escape the murderers in the middle of the worst blizzard in centuries… and she was only 5!

Fast forward twelve years and Bobbi Jo dreams of starting a new life away from the trauma of her past and the antipathy of pitiless relatives.

The nightmare isn't over… but perhaps the tables have turned…

Vindicta - when death isn't retribution enough…

Corrupt Covenant

with Rori Bleu

A pledge of eternal peace and prosperity sounds too good to refuse… unless, of course, the pledge comes from an immortal dragon.

A contract established in exchange for a king's life and the protection of his lineage *should* have expired when a desperate queen, facing hordes baying for her destruction, loses faith in the oath... but evil has a long memory.

Trapped for a millennium in a sarcophagus at the bottom of the Danube, death lay beyond the queen's grasp until the day nature, fate, and a mysterious archaeologist joined forces to dredge her from her grave.

A life revived. A liegeman doomed to be reborn until he saves his queen. A dragon who has not forgiven an act of betrayal.

Can two souls, separated for a millennium, break the corrupt covenant, or are they fated to dance to the dragon's tune, for eternity?

The Sela Helsdatter Saga

with Rori Bleu

A Flip of the Coin - Book One

What happens in Helheim *never* stays in Helheim.

Sela Helsdatter wishes it would. Punished for allowing her quest for power to rule her actions, she has endured eons of torment. The flip of a coin seems to offer some hope of redemption but, tasked with ridding the world of her erstwhile captor *and* lover, escape does not mean freedom.

No problem for a warrior queen… right? Wrong! Sela is no longer in ninth century Norðvegr, but twenty-first century New York with all its challenges, and where slightest misstep could spell her doom.

Aided by the most unlikely hero, Sela scours the city for her adversary, who delights in taunting her, determined to drag her back to Hell.

Will she prevail, or will A Flip of the Coin catapult her back to the abyss?

Conceived Chaos - Book Two

After ridding the world of her tormentor, and finding the love of her life,

Sela Helsdatter could be forgiven for thinking she deserves a little peace.

No such luck!

Marriage to the God of Mischief is a walk in the park compared with the terror about to be unleashed from Valhalla. A diabolical edict from Odin himself sees the nine months pregnant, Sela fleeing from the entire Norse pantheon — with no clue why.

A price on her head and a target on her belly, the only person she can trust is her husband, who is keeping her in the dark. Does her unborn child hold the key to this Conceived Chaos?

Odin's Bane - Book Three

Sela Helsdatter cannot catch a break. Relentless in his jealousy and wrath, Odin is determined that neither Sela nor her infant daughter will survive.

Shattered by loss, and with no time to grieve, Sela has to rely on the one person she believes responsible for her current predicament.

A lost friendship revived, the disparate trio seek refuge in a remote corner of Montana, with the uneasy awareness the child may be the key to their salvation.

Vowing Odin will not harm a hair on her daughter's head, Sela has to use every trick at her disposal to thwart the Norse Deity. At the same time another fiendish subversion threatens the future of humanity.

Will Odin be victorious… or is another power stirring which will prove to be his bane?

Arcane Alchemy

Freya's Fate: A Helsdatter Novella

What happens when the goddess of seduction and love finds herself on the losing end of a romance...to a human no less? She packs up, summons her carriage, and sets off to unravel a mystery which has intrigued her for eons.

An odyssey to far flung lands brings the answer tantalisingly close.

Only to be snatched away... for Freya's fate is inextricably linked to the one person she is determined to avoid and, to ignore the not-so-subtle summons for help will lead to tragedy.

Prowling on the periphery, a baleful deity prepares to pounce and, as ever when gods interfere in the lives of mortals, chaos ensues.

It will take more than a touch of arcane alchemy to avert the looming catastrophe.

Regency Romance

Once Upon An Earl

Linen and Lace - Book One

When Fate saw fit to intervene in the life of Giles Trevallier, the very respectable Earl of Winchester, by dropping a female — soaked to the skin and with no memory of who she is or how she came to be there — literally at his feet, no one could have predicted the outcome.

While uncovering her identity, Giles realises he is falling hopelessly in love with his mystery guest, who unbeknownst to him, is succumbing to similar emotions; but, when the heart is involved, a thoughtless word or gesture can thwart even Fate's best-laid plans.

Faced with misunderstandings, whispers of scandal, secret documents and foreign agents, their chance at a happy ever after seems elusive, but fairy tales often happen when least expected, and love — however inconvenient — usually finds a way to conquer all.

To Unlock Her Heart

Linen and Lace - Book Two

Abused by a duke, and shunned by Society, relief seems at hand when Grace Aldeburgh is bequeathed a house in a small village, far from malicious gossips.

Once there, a tentative friendship blooms between Grace and Theo Elliott, the local doctor, who has already resolved to be the man to unlock her heart.

Just when happiness appears to be within her grasp, her erstwhile tormentor once again stalks Grace. After a failed kidnap attempt, the duke's quest culminates in an acrimonious confrontation, and the reason for his venal pursuit becomes agonisingly clear.

Love on a Winter's Tide

Linen and Lace - Book Three

Every day, Helena disappears into a world few acknowledge, helping the poor, downtrodden, and abused. A husband is the last thing she can be bothered with.

Busy managing his shipping line, Hugh Drummond sees no need for a wife, whose only joy is dancing and frivolity. If — and it was a huge if — he ever married, it would be to a woman as capable as he, not some giddy society Miss.

Then, Hugh meets Helena and despite their resolve, fate, it seems, has other ideas. As their attraction deepens however, treachery threatens to tear them apart. Will they uncover the perpetrator in time, or will their love be swept away, lost forever on a winter's tide?

A Love Unquenchable

Linen and Lace - Book Four

Jessica Drummond, a bright and cheerful young woman, rarely gives romance, let alone love, a thought. Long hours working in her brother's shipping office affords little chance of her ever meeting an eligible bachelor.

Duncan Barrington, veteran of the Napoleonic Wars, believes himself wounded in both body and soul. He has no intention of inflicting his demons on anyone, certainly not a beautiful and, in his opinion, irresponsible city lady.

One cold and snowy morning, the plight of a bedraggled puppy throws Jessica and Duncan together and, as a spark of something indefinable yet wholly unquenchable begins to burn, it is unclear who rescued whom.

A Hidden Rose

Linen and Lace - Book Five

After witnessing his mother's grief at the loss of his father, Nick

Drummond resolved never to cause someone he loved such distress. Even the happiness of his siblings would not sway him — until he met Rose.

Rose Archer was almost content assisting her doctor father in a tiny fishing village in the north of Yorkshire. To experience the world beyond, a tantalising dream — until she met Nick.

Unexpectedly, the impossible becomes possible, and the renounced — desired above all things, but the shipwreck that brought them together, may yet tear them apart. Will Nick learn to trust his heart, or will his love for Rose remain forever hidden

The Daffodil Garden

Horrifically scarred during the war, William Harcourt - Marquis of Blackthorne - prefers to spend his days in the quiet of his daffodil garden; plants do not pity, turn away, or judge.

Lucy Truscott, whose life is far removed from that of the *ton*, has no idea that by saving the life of a young woman, to whom she bears an uncanny resemblance, her own will be placed in mortal danger.

A chance encounter leads to something more. William begins to trust that Lucy sees the man beneath the scars, while Lucy is persuaded that love might actually transcend status.

Unfortunately, before their courtship has really begun, someone has every intention of ending it - permanently.

The Unconventional Duchess

Refusing to suffer the humiliation of her husband flaunting his mistress at Society events, the newly married Duchess of Wallingstead, Ella

Lennox, takes control of her life. She leaves London for the family's country seat in remote Yorkshire.

A woman alone, Ella spends the next four years turning a cold, grim house into a home, and transforming the fortunes of the estate. Not afraid of hard work, she soon earns the respect of those around her with her determination and unconventional attitude.

Out of the blue, the duke arrives. Resigned to another arduous visit, Ella is stunned when it seems he is attempting to court her.

Impossible!

Could her dream of a happy marriage be about to come true?

Everything hangs on a snowstorm, a herd of cows and an uninvited guest!

Rescuing Her Knight

The *de Wiltons* — Book One

A story, invented to keep a little girl distracted, marks the beginning of another tale. One destined to remain unfinished for twenty years.

At thirteen, Adam Marchmain became Kitty de Wilton's 'Knight of the Garden' — a title bestowed following an accident which resulted in six-year-old Kitty having her knee sutured. Kitty never forgot his gallantry, but pledges made as children rarely survive into adulthood.

Their paths separated until Fate decreed, they meet again.

Widowed, badly disfigured and his sight ruined, Adam returns to his family home, a shadow of his former self.

Similarly afflicted, although her scars are invisible, Kitty — against her better judgement — is persuaded to help Adam banish his demons. This requires a subterfuge which, if discovered, might shatter more than the bonds of friendship forged two decades previously.

To Kitty, determined to break through the shield Adam has erected, the risk is worth it.

To see his smile and hear his laughter.

To rescue the knight of her childhood.

Just when a fairy tale ending is within her grasp, Kitty is threatened by the man who murdered her husband. In a cruel twist the tables are turned, and Kitty is the one who needs rescuing.

Elusive Hearts

An Unexpected Romance - Book One

What happens when two people whose elusive hearts fight an indefinable attraction, neither looked for nor desired, dare to dream?

When her fiancé and sister abscond to Gretna Green on her wedding day, Sapphira Beresford longs to escape, to avoid the gossipmongers gloating over her misfortune. Disillusioned, she is determined not to be burnt again, swearing off romance and marriage.

A fortuitous invitation sees her embarking on a journey to Pompeii where she meets Leofwin Colleville, reclusive marquis, amateur antiquarian, and her host for the duration.

Although enamoured of the ruins gradually being unearthed and ecstatic to have the opportunity to assist, Sapphira is troubled by her host's attitude, which blows hot and cold.

A confirmed bachelor, Leofwin Colleville is happiest surrounded by ancient ruins, and would prefer to brave the whole of Napoleon's armies alone, than face a lady on the hunt for a husband. The arrival of an unexpected guest throws his unencumbered existence into turmoil, but the harder he strives to maintain his distance, the more she gets under his skin.

Sparks fly and, as Leofwin's truculence undermines Sapphira's already battered confidence, her adventure of a lifetime seems doomed to disaster.

Until the day she runs afoul of greedy treasure hunters.

In the aftermath what was scorned becomes the one thing they crave above all else, but when it comes to the heart, nothing is ever simple.

His Fiery Hoyden

A Novella

Livvy has no respect for the nobility; they let her down when she most needed them. Why should she accede to their demands now?

Philip, Lord Harrington, is stunned to discover the young heir to the dukedom lives a stone's throw away in a ramshackle cottage, and resolves to restore the child to his birthright.

They meet in a clash of wills, but just when it seems Livvy might surrender, the victory Philip desires, may not taste all that sweet.

A Regency Duet

Luck be a Pirate

Luck wasn't something retired pirate Kennet Alexson believed in — good or bad. However, even he had to concede that landing a job at Trentams shipyard, and meeting Lynette Collins, was more than coincidence.

Fortune it seemed, was smiling on him for once.

As Kennet adjusts to life on dry land, his friendship with Lynette deepens into something far more enduring, and what once seemed elusive now becomes possible.

Unfortunately, fate has other plans, and Kennet's good luck is about to run out.

The Highwayman's Kiss

Surrendered Hearts — Book One

Nothing exciting had ever happened to Juliette St Clair. Her days were spent assisting her father or calling on friends, wandering art galleries, taking constitutionals or, and more preferably, escaping into her books. Her evenings her evenings — an endless round of balls, where she preferred to remain invisible.

Until the day she was robbed by a highwayman.

A Regency Christmas Double

Heart Rescued

Four years since Jasper lost the woman he was hoping to marry. Four years since he closed his heart and withdrew from Society. He has no idea his reclusive existence is about to be shattered.

Enter his sister's best friend, Harriet, a flame haired beauty, who needs his help.

Reluctantly he agrees and as they spend time together, it is clear their feelings run deep. Although Harriet affects Jasper in a way no woman ever has, he believes her to be out of his league ~ but it's Christmas and she might just be the one to melt his frozen heart

Catch a Snowflake

Romance often blossoms in the most unlikely of places - but in a ward full of wounded soldiers - surely not?

When Lucas Withers comes face to face with Jemima Parsons - a young woman who blames him for her brother's injury - falling in love is the last thing on their minds. What neither of them anticipated, was the magic of snowflakes.

Fate is Curious

A Novella

Happily, ever after? No such thing! Bereft, following her beloved husband's sudden death, Lady Charlotte Sherbrooke has lost her belief in romantic nonsense.

Successful shipping merchant, Zacharie Romain, is no stranger to loss; his business can be hazardous. Moreover, his wife died in childbirth and even though it happened a decade ago, he has no mind to expose himself to such sorrow again.

They meet in less than joyful circumstances but, as the year turns and grief diminishes, the woes of a small boy become the catalyst for something wholly unexpected. Can Charlotte and Zacharie trust what Fate has in store or will past heartbreak prevent them from taking a chance on love?

A Christmas Prayer

with Ashlee Shades

A Short Story

An entreaty from a frightened child.

Orphaned and only nine, Caroline Thorne has to grow up before her time. She is doing everything she can to keep what is left of her family together and out of the workhouse but is terrified her prayers are not being heard. Or maybe they are…

A petition from a woman desperate for a family.

A chance meeting with three orphaned siblings, tugs at Elizabeth Barrington's heart strings. Thus far, she and her husband have not been blessed with children and, as Christmas approaches, a plan begins to form - one which might just be the answer to her prayers.

Two Christmas prayers, as different as they are the same.

Will they hear and, more importantly, heed the answer?

The Lady's Wager

Surrendered Hearts- Book Two

A Novelette

Ged Mowbray will do anything to avoid being married off to the suitable prospects his parents insist on parading in front of him.

Melissa Bouchard is under no illusion her sizeable dowry is the attraction to suitors, not her.

An overheard conversation leads to an offer too good to refuse, but what happens when a lady's wager, becomes a gamble on the happily ever after, you did not even realise you wanted?

Winning Emma

Surrendered Hearts - Book Three

A Novelette

Randolph Craythorpe — earl, covert operative, and occasional highwayman — believed his dalliance with Lady Felicity Hartwich would lead to marriage. It did, but not to him! The arrival of an unwelcome guest, however, provides the perfect opportunity to indulge in a little retaliation.

Emma Newbury accompanies her cousin, Lady Charity Anscombe, to London for the Christmas season. Once there, she comes face to face with the three men who witnessed the humiliating aftermath of her father's disgrace — one of whom, to her irritation, has taken up residence in her dreams.

Their infrequent encounters only serve to confuse but, while winter tightens its grip on the city, what was inconceivable becomes the one thing for which they both yearn, yet bound by Society's rules, cannot admit.

As the snow falls, Randolph begins to understand that to win Emma, he will have to surrender.

Moonbeams and Mistletoe

Surrendered Hearts – Book Four

A Novelette

If we are part of a universe where moonbeams and mistletoe exist, nothing is insurmountable for, otherwise, what is the point?

To Emily Livingston, spinster — this deceptively frivolous phrase was all she had left of her betrothed.

To Henry Bartholomew, widower — the sentiment, while naïve, also serves as a reminder that even in the darkest of hours, light can be found… it was simply a matter of perspective.

When four-year-old twins run into Emily — literally — she has no idea where their unexpected encounter will lead. Determined to ensure his children are *not* being schooled into something nefarious, Henry resolves to meet this mysterious lady who has enthralled the duo with her stories.

One dull and otherwise ordinary autumnal morning, two disparate souls are brought together, and long-forgotten emotions are stirred.

The question is whether Henry and Emily have the courage to follow their hearts or be forever trapped in the sadness of the past. Can moonbeams and mistletoe persuade them, the answer was there all along?

A Love Impossible

A Regency M/M Novelette

Tasked with investigating a heinous crime, Edward Lindsay travels from London to Dublin — a city which holds too many memories — in the guise of guardian to his sister. He knew it could be hazardous, and relished the challenge, but that wasn't what caused his stomach to tighten as they approached landfall.

Dublin held more than just a murderer.

There was also Aidan.

While attending a party, Aidan Griffen is astonished when he comes face to face with a man who fled Dublin two years previously. A man he has desperately tried to forget.

As Edward closes in on his quarry, a fire, deliberately extinguished, is rekindled. But what of it? Edward and Aidan share a love impossible, and to acknowledge their feelings — more dangerous than confronting a killer.

Is there any hope of a happily ever after?

Unravelling Roana

A Regency Novelette

Tired of being ignored by her husband, Roana Dumont, Countess of Brooketon does the one thing guaranteed to get his attention. She runs away… to Venice, leaving behind a set of riddles for him to solve… *if* he feels their marriage is worth saving.

Gideon Dumont, 6th Earl of Brooketon is flabbergasted when he discovers his wife has apparently vanished off the face of the earth. A series of puzzles, the only clue as to her whereabouts.

The question is… will he unravel them?

Love Kindled

A Regency Novelette

Recently widowed, Amelia Ingram - Countess of Gresham, decides to shake off the fetters from her arranged and loveless marriage. Exploiting her new-found independence, Amelia indulges her yearning to explore - incognito.

Her ploy works so well, she receives an offer of employment from the dangerously handsome, Rupert Latimer - Earl of Badlesmere. On impulse, she accepts and finds herself governess to Cate, a delightful scamp of a child. What began as a bit of a game on Amelia's part, evolves into something far more profound, and a flame she presumed impossible to ignite, is kindled.

An unexpected turn of events leads to yet another offer. This time there is far more at stake and, determined history not repeat itself, Amelia confesses her ruse.

Rupert has been burnt once. Will he douse the spark, or take a risk and trust his heart?

Fairy Tale Romances

Chasing Bluebells

A Fairy Tale Novella

Once upon a time, somewhere in France, there was a man whose reckless obsession led him down a dark path — one which, ultimately, cost him his life. That ought to have been the end of it. Regrettably, as is so often the case, those who least deserve it, suffer for the actions of others.

A decade after being sent away, Sebastien Daviau returns to the little village where everything began. Hoping to lay the ghosts of his childhood to rest, he studiously ignores the possibility, he might run into Charlotte de Montbeliard.

As luck would have it, Charlotte is the one who runs into him... well, his horse... and although the brief encounter leaves a lasting impression, neither recognises the other.

A name revealed causes a freak accident, catapulting Sebastien's past into his present, and bringing him face to face with a man whose reputation would intimidate the most ardent of suitors.

Can whatever is blossoming between Charlotte and Sebastien survive the challenge imposed, or is their happily ever after about to fade as quickly as the bluebells they loved to chase?

Contemporary Romance

Of Ruins and Romance

Kassandra Winters has intrigued Gabriel St Germain since he accidentally knocked her flying outside her university professor's office. Her face haunts his dreams, yet he never expected to see her again. So, he is surprised when she appears, as though destined to do so, in the middle of a ruin, and he concocts a plan to win her heart.

Gabriel's old-fashioned courtship touches something deep inside Kassie and, although struggling to believe someone as handsome as Gabriel could possibly be interested in her, she soon realises she has fallen irrevocably in love with him. However, just as Kassie shares everything of herself with Gabriel, her world comes crashing down.

Can their romance survive, or will it fall in ruins, like the relics of antiquity that brought them together?

All At Once It's You

When Alex arrives in the small village of Rosedale Abbey, to take up a position as a research assistant for a renowned archaeologist, the last thing she is looking for, or expects to find, is love.

Jake was perfectly happy with the status quo. When it came to relationships, he didn't do committed or long term. He called the shots, and if his current flame didn't like it, she knew what to do. A philosophy, which served him well - until he met Alex.

Romance blooms, but even as the untamed wilderness of the North Yorkshire moors weaves its spell, a long-buried secret might yet jeopardise their happily ever after.

Cobweb Dreams

A Novella

A holiday on the Scottish isle of Mull was just the break Chloe Shepherd needed, an escape from her boring office job and her complete lack of anything resembling a social life. Romance, it seems, isn't on the cards and, although Chloe dreams of finding her soulmate she is beginning to believe love is like cobwebs — spun overnight, only to vanish in the early morning breeze.

Under sufferance, Dominic Winters makes a flying visit to Mull to check on a rental property owned by his family. He hasn't got time for this — so indulging in a holiday fling is the last thing on his mind.

A lamb stuck in a bog proves a most unexpected matchmaker and, while Mull weaves its magic, Chloe wonders whether those fragile cobwebs might be far more stubborn than she thought.

Just One Step

A Short Story

In the aftermath of an horrific car accident, Daisy Forrester travels to Italy - hoping, so far from her memories, she might begin to heal.

Archaeologist, and single father, Adam Willoughby is too busy looking after his young daughter to give romance let alone love, a thought.

Neither expects a chance encounter in an ancient ruin to be anything more, but sometimes, that's all it takes.

His Heart's Second Sigh

A Novella

Reuben Faulkner and Paige Latimer are two happily single people, who have no desire to upset the status quo.

Unexpectedly, they are thrown together, only to discover both want far more than a casual friendship.

Just when things take an interesting turn, Reuben's past catches up with them, and threatens to derail their blossoming romance before it has chance to start.